THE CURSED CASTLE

DARK RELICS SERIES
BOOK 2

RON RIPLEY

EDITED BY ANNE LAO
AND DAWN KLEMISH

ISBN: 979-8-89476-296-8
Copyright © 2025 by ScareStreet.com

Enter the Realm of Terror…

We'd like to take a moment to thank you for your support and invite you to join our VIP newsletter.

Dive deeper into the darkness with exclusive offers, early access to new releases, and bone-chilling deals when you sign up at www.ScareStreet.com.

Let the nightmares begin…

See you in the shadows,
Scare Street

SCOTLAND, 1498

John Lambert mopped his brow with a dirty rag and looked down at his handiwork. It was not impressive. Four hours of sweat and toil, and he'd penetrated only about four feet down. The soil was heavy and black with moisture. Lambert was being paid by the hour, of course, not by results. But Lambert was no fool. The Scots laird who had hired him and the other English workmen might balk at paying for nothing but a few empty trenches.

Lambert looked at his fellow diggers. All the workmen had been recruited down in England, just across the border, by one of the laird's servants. They had been lured to this bleak part of the border country with the promise of steady work, free meals, and a place to sleep. The steady work part had been true, at least. The meals had proved less than appetizing, and the accommodation was an old pigsty with a leaking roof. But there was free beer, and that quelled the grumbling for a while.

Before the first day's work was out, one of the hired men had heard a rumor from a kitchen skivvy. Laird Angus McIvor, strapped for cash like most of the minor nobility, had sought advice from a witch. She was the one who had advised plundering the mound for treasure. Lambert knew witches often leagued with the devil against the godly. Advice from such creatures was apt to lead men astray.

Then there was the job itself. Digging into an old burial mound was common enough, but those who did it seldom unearthed anything of value. Earlier generations had had much the same notion and plundered all the good stuff. Or so Lambert thought. However, the laird held that this particular mound had remained untouched. And if there was treasure, the workers would get a share. A small share, of course, but something. For a working man down on his luck, that was Lambert's best offer in months.

Lambert and his six companions had started vigorously enough, cutting trenches across the shallow mound and going down to ground level. Opinions varied as to who might be buried in the grassy hummock. Some said a vanquished Roman general lay there. Others held that the grave belonged to a Viking prince. One man even claimed that they would unearth King Arthur himself.

Lambert, who had had some schooling courtesy of a kindly priest, thought none of those ideas plausible, but he could offer no alternative. The origins of these ancient graves were lost in the mists of time. And who cared, anyway? Money was all that mattered.

That was four days ago. The mound was now crisscrossed with trenches, and nothing had been unearthed. All optimism gone, the workmen labored on grimly. The pittance they were getting was better than nothing, which was what awaited them back in England. Another outbreak of the plague had left thousands destitute.

A few spots of rain were falling. Lambert looked up at the dark clouds scudding overhead. A little rain was fine—it cooled a man down—but he didn't like the idea of working in a torrential downpour. He wondered if the unseasonal weather had been why locals hadn't wanted this job. Then, he dismissed the idea. The Scots were a fractious and drunken rabble; every true-born Englishman knew that. His uncle had lost four head of cattle to border raiders just weeks ago. But you couldn't call a Scotsman work shy. And yet, not one local wanted to earn a few shillings digging up the mound.

Remembering that he was leaning on his shovel, Lambert looked back at the castle to see if his skiving was being observed. As if summoned by the thought, a dark-clad figure appeared in the arched gateway and began to walk across the moat. Angus, Laird McIvor, was a tall, broad-shouldered man with an impressive mane of red hair and a beard to match. Not a man you could easily mistake at a distance. Lambert picked up his shovel and started digging again. The laird had eyes like a hawk and might have seen him slacking.

The blade of the shovel struck something. There was no sound, but the impact shock traveled up the wooden shaft. Probably just another lump of rock, but it was worth a look. Lambert set down his shovel and crouched in the bottom of the trench. A rounded, dark-brown object protruded slightly from the side of his trench. He pulled it out and felt a shiver of apprehension. It was a skull, and its jawless, empty sockets seemed to stare at him in mute reproof.

Lambert's grandmother had told him stories about men who disturbed graves and of the dire vengeance of ghosts. He didn't want any visitations in the small hours. But the more practical side of his nature told him that the dead stayed dead. In Lambert's experience, it was the living you had to watch out for. He threw the skull onto the grassy slope and then scrabbled in the dirt for a few moments to uncover the upper portion of a skeleton, now headless.

Lambert was no scholar. Book learning was for the clergy. But this was plainly a respected man buried with some precious items. A large brooch gleamed alluringly, even on this dull day. Gold, without a doubt. Lambert saw the remains of the cloak the brooch had held in place. There was also a long, slender object clutched to the chest of the nameless dead man. It was wrapped in some kind of leather binding. There were rings on the skeletal fingers, too.

Silver and gold, Lambert thought. *Enough precious metal to buy all the beer in this godforsaken county. Or invest in a flock of good, healthy ewes.*

"What have you found?"

Lambert looked up to see the laird standing on the edge of the trench. Some of the other workmen were also looking on but didn't dare approach McIvor too closely. The man's reputation was not as dark as most border lords, but the man cut an imposing figure. McIvor had the slightly bow-legged gait of an accomplished horseman and the muscular, uneven shoulders of a man who regularly practiced with a longsword.

Lambert gestured.

"I found a man long dead, my lord. And something of value, perhaps. Mayhap a prince's treasure if fortune smiles upon us!"

The Englishman hoped the word "us" had not gone unnoticed.

"Aye, I see it," growled McIvor, hunkering down. "Pass it up to me, man!"

Lambert removed the brooch, which McIvor examined and then quickly pocketed.

"And now, would that be a sword he's holding? Let me see it!"

The laird jumped into the trench, and Lambert stepped aside. He watched as the Scotsman bent and detached the dead man's fingers from the leather binding and picked up the find. A sudden gust of wind startled Lambert, bringing with it a stench like rotten flesh. Lambert gagged on the carrion stink, almost doubling over. After the vile odor had passed, he heard a voice whispering urgently in a language he did not understand. Disoriented, it took him a moment to realize that the laird was standing motionless, eyes blank as if daydreaming.

"My lord? Is anything wrong?"

"Wrong?"

McIvor's pale blue eyes focused on Lambert. The huge hands were unwrapping the sword, and rotten leather strips fell away to reveal bright metal. It was an impressive weapon but strange in design. Lambert had done his time as a mercenary and knew a little about swords. This one had an elaborate gilded hilt and a long grip, but it lacked the curved knuckle guard. The blade was like a drastically elongated leaf, broadest in the middle, tapering toward both the hilt and the point.

"A fine old sword, sire," Lambert said, feeling the urge to break the silence.

"Aye. Old. So very old," whispered the laird as if talking to himself.

Angus hefted the unwrapped weapon for a moment and then swung it with practiced ease in a flashing arc. Lambert flinched and tried to step away, but the trench wall stopped him. An icy chill pierced his throat, followed by a sensation of warmth. He looked down to see his lifeblood gushing forth like a fountain, splashing his boots, the dirt, and the garments of the laird. The pounding of blood in his ears grew louder while the world around him darkened. He heard shouts and screams of panic and anger, but they came from a great distance.

The last thing he remembered as he lay on the muddy floor of the trench was a deluge of blood falling onto him like rain.

The warmth was strangely comforting.

CHAPTER 1
HARD TO SAY GOODBYE

On the morning Leroy left for good, Craig Ellison was woken by Smokey Robinson and the Miracles. Not their ghosts, just one of their classic tracks. He waited until the final bars of *Tears of a Clown* had faded, relishing the song until the last drop. Before befriending Leroy, he had been ignorant of a long, rich chapter in American culture.

Craig wondered what else Leroy might have cast light upon, given time. But it was too late now. For good or ill, the moment of decision had come, and the ghost had chosen a new path.

Craig unstuck his eyelids, got out of bed, and padded barefoot into the bathroom. The face he saw in the mirror was pale and maybe a little chubby. A girl had once told Craig that he had nice eyes, and he had clung to that notion ever since. He smiled, remembering the girl's gentleness, and her patience with him, skipping over how that relationship had ended. He tried not to look at his narrow shoulders and spreading waistline, but it was hard to avoid the conclusion that he was out of shape. Or just the wrong shape. Either would do.

Craig decided to shave. Some days, he didn't bother. It wasn't as if he had a regular job, with an office of people scrutinizing him. But this was a special occasion. He lathered up and did the easy bits first, drawing the razor over his cheeks. Then, he moved on to the trickier slopes of his neck and chin. He was just tackling his septum when a huge, tattooed biker appeared in the mirror behind him.

"Ouch!" Craig nicked his nose with the blade.

"Sorry, buddy," said Billy, not sounding sorry at all. The ghost took a childlike pleasure in startling his landlord now and again.

Craig wiped the pink foam off his upper lip.

"I think I'll live."

In death as in life, Billy looked like the sort of guy no sane person would mess with. Craig sometimes wished he could be so intimidating. But, thanks to Billy's many stories, he grasped that being the big, scary guy came with its share of problems.

As Craig brushed his hair, Billy asked him if he was ready.

"As I'll ever be," Craig replied. "It's a question of whether Leroy is ready."

"He seems kind of pumped, talking about the will of the Lord and stuff," the ghost said with dry amusement. "I think he expects St. Peter to roll out the red carpet or something. But you never know; he might back out."

"We'll see," Craig said. "Now, can I please get dressed without an audience?"

He put on casuals, slippers, and the charm that Tara Pride had given him. The viking compass, she had called it. *Vegvisir.* The metal disk was inscribed with Runic symbols that supposedly helped a lost traveler find their way home. In the age of Google Maps, that might seem redundant. But Craig knew from experience that there was more than one way to be lost. Since adolescence, he'd become an expert on not knowing where to go next.

Craig stepped into his cramped living room to wish his more civilized lodgers good morning. The support group he had formed a few years ago had once been far larger. But his "talking cure" approach to moving on had painstakingly whittled it down to three. Billy, massive and obdurate, had never expressed the slightest desire to leave the earthly plane. He enjoyed watching people screw up and indulged in a fair amount of voyeurism. Chloe, the emo girl, was reluctant to talk about anything, and that went double for moving on.

This left Leroy, once a conscientious building super and handyman, whose proudest moment had been marching in Washington with Dr. King. Leroy was the most talkative and supportive of the three. Craig would miss him. He had lost friends and lovers so often in the past. Most people struggled with the fact that he saw ghosts and talked to them. Logically, he should've suppressed his power and lived a normal life. But even if that were possible, Craig could not see himself doing it. He liked helping ghosts. He felt that everyone needed a friend, in death as in life.

Which led to another paradox. He had dedicated his spare time to losing the ghosts who had become his friends. Doing the right thing was the point, though, not having fun. Or so he told himself often. He had chosen a good path, and he had to follow it.

"Hey, the main man!" said Leroy, his smile dazzling.

Craig always felt the urge to high-five Leroy. It was one of the drawbacks of having friends who were dead. He'd recently come across the Japanese term "skinship", instantly feeling that it was one thing he needed. Physical contact. Flesh to flesh. Not necessarily something sexual, just the touch of another live human being.

"Hey, don't sweat it, buddy," Leroy said, serious now.

"I'm okay," Craig said, letting the ghost misinterpret his expression. "I'll be fine after breakfast."

Billy seemed content to look on without commenting as Craig made his usual breakfast, eggs over easy on toast. On this special day, he treated himself to one rasher of bacon and some decent coffee instead of the instant stuff. His ghost tours had been going well, and his last job for Peregrine Stark had been very lucrative. In general, things seemed to be on the up.

So, why do I feel so unsure of myself?

The answer was obvious. Since he'd acquired his new power at Grendon Mill, Craig had moved on several ghosts he'd known next to nothing about. It was easy with strangers, but Leroy had been a friend for years, a kindhearted dead man sharing Craig's life. All paranormal powers involved the user's thoughts and feelings. You could screw up massively by being too emotional, or not emotionally invested enough, and Craig felt conflicted about Leroy leaving.

"I'm not sure if I can do it," he blurted out.

Sitting opposite him at the apartment's one small table, Leroy shrugged as if it were a minor issue.

"Hey, if it works it works. If not, well, I guess it's not so bad around here."

Craig finished mopping up yolk with the last bite of toast and then wiped his mouth with a paper napkin. Chloe was not visible at the moment, but her quiet presence had, from the outset, made him less of a slob. Such, he reflected, was the power of any feminine presence. It was like having a security camera combined with an etiquette coach.

"Well, time's a-wastin'," Leroy observed, standing up. "How do you want me, my friend?"

As he stood, Craig struggled to find the right words.

"I just want to say… I mean, it's been great, all these years. So much good advice. Kindness is so underrated. Heck, I'm saying I'll… I'll miss you."

Leroy stepped around the table—he was always careful like that, never walking through solid objects—and held out his arms. It was a fake hug, distance maintained, but Craig still appreciated it. Then, to his surprise, Billy spoke up.

"I'll miss you too, fella," the biker growled. "I'll have to get my moral guidance from Craig from now on."

That got them all laughing, and the tension, while not quite dispelled, was eased. Craig stood up straight and looked Leroy in the eye. Then, he started to focus his mind on the task at hand. Street noise, the fading aroma of coffee, and a twinge of indigestion from eating too quickly were pushed aside until the world consisted of two men in a room, facing one another.

The long-dead psychic Alva Gates had taught him what to do. Craig focused on the image of a door that could be opened. A threshold that could be crossed. So long as that was clear, and the ghost wanted to move on, it should work. At first, it seemed that things would work out as they had before.

The first sign was a tingling sensation somewhere between a mild cramp and static electricity. The feeling ran over Craig's skin, tiny hairs rising and falling in waves. Then came the vortex, forming swiftly above Leroy's head. It was a small whirlpool of blue-white light, faint at first, and then growing brighter until it shone with almost dazzling intensity.

"Holy sh—"

Billy's whispered remark caused a glitch in Craig's concentration, but he refocused and held his mind steady. Leroy looked up, his amiable features lit by the eerie glow. Then, it happened. Filaments of energy flickered out from the ghost to encircle Craig, and in an instant, the small apartment was gone. Instead, he saw a huge face looking down at him, and a warm voice speaking Leroy's name. A mother leaning over her child's crib. Now, he was out in a backyard where a little girl, cute in a pink dress, threw a ball. He deliberately fumbled the catch and did a pratfall. The laughter from the girl was the most wonderful sound he had ever heard. Another shift of scene. Now, a man was speaking, a familiar face and voice, as Craig stood in a vast crowd. Dr. King in Washington. The scene changed again and again, emotions rising and falling, faces laughing and weeping, momentous changes, and trivial details vying for his attention. Craig knew what it was to fall in love, to become a proud father, and to feel the terrible despair as death tore him from a brave woman, the weeping child. Craig was riding a roller coaster of Leroy's memories, embraced by the man's soul.

And he was rising toward the portal.

Craig realized the danger just in time and nearly lost control. He stopped just short of the whirlpool of light, which felt warm and welcoming. Leroy was already passing through. Craig sensed gratitude, which was then lost in a wondrous outburst of joy, and the image of Leroy's mother returned.

Then, Craig was standing in his living room again. Billy and Chloe were looking on. The girl was sobbing. Billy looked at his feet.

"Guess it worked," the big guy said.

"Guess so."

Craig sat heavily and blew his nose on his napkin. He felt drained of emotion and energy. The apartment he had tried to make cheerful for his friends as much as himself now seemed colorless; a place of drabness and clutter.

His phone pinged.

Some instinct told him who the message was from before he checked.

"Stark," he said flatly.

Billy emitted a snort of amusement.

"That convoluted SOB. Wonder how he's gonna try and get ya killed this time."

Chapter 2
DEMONCORE

The band was called Ashtaroth's Auntie, but that hadn't prevented them from building a fan base. The venue was packed solid with dark-clad youngsters, sweating, yelling, and jumping up and down in lieu of dancing. T-shirts and other merch were evidence. The band's logo was based around the initials AA. It seemed the more famous AA was cool with this or, more likely, didn't know.

The band's music could best be described as deafening, derivative, and doom-laden. Power chords and bellowed lyrics resounded from the corrugated tin roof of a long-disused warehouse. The effect, Tara Pride thought, was how she imagined a plane crash would feel if the impact could somehow last for more than an hour.

I'm too old for this.

It was a depressing notion, but everyone around her seemed to be ten years younger. Jiggling puppy fat was on show in abundance. So were vain attempts to grow goatees on acne-ridden chins. Various drinks were being spilled by accident or deliberately slung around. Tara was sticky all over. She wondered if heat stroke would claim her before the real action began.

If it ever did.

A scientist by training, Tara had taken a long time to get used to ambiguity, riddles, and omens. But she was being paid by the parents of a girl who had vanished at or near a gig by Ashtaroth's Auntie. At first, Tara, while sympathetic, had felt nothing supernatural involved. But then, a contact at the police department had leaked something to a journalist, who had in turn sent Tara an MP4 file. With the file had come a message:

Too weird for the cops; they're ignoring it. My editor thinks
it's a deepfake. See what you think.

Someone had live-streamed the band's previous gig. As usual, amateur filming yielded amateurish results, and at first, Tara had no idea why her informant had bothered. However, she watched the video with the sound turned well down. She noticed something unusual at the halfway mark.

The band's frontman—who went by the moniker Evil Jethro— had been prancing around the stage, microphone in hand, yelling something about the Pleiades. Tara smiled at that. The Pleiades were a group of young, hot stars in the constellation Taurus, and she had written an academic paper about them a few years back. What the star cluster had to do with Ashtaroth's Auntie and their nihilistic yammering was not clear.

The screen was suddenly obscured by a snow of interference. To Tara, this signified a powerful energy pulse nearby. When the digital blizzard cleared, the lead singer was standing motionless with his hands at his sides. The rest of the band had adopted the same inert pose, their faces blank.

After scrutinizing every pixel, she'd concluded that it might be fake, but it was still worth checking out in person, because the more digging she did, the more fans of that particular band seemed to vanish. Every now and then, after Ashtaroth's Auntie played a gig, somebody never got home. And yet, there was no shred of evidence to suggest foul play. No witnesses to an abduction, no last-minute calls or texts asking for help, and no bodies found. Nothing.

Tara snapped out of her reverie. The gig had reached a hiatus. Evil Jethro and the band had stopped playing. All except for the lead guitarist, who was posing while the speakers blasted out a long, dissonant screech. Then he, too, fell silent. Now, all the band members were motionless and looking down at the stage. The crowd around Tara grew restive. Catcalling and whistles merged with ironic cheers.

Tara reached inside her voluminous cargo pants and took out one of her concealed weapons. She was not sure what was about to happen, because the phone footage had been so poor. But in that messy video, she had glimpsed something fascinating near the stage.

The crowd fell silent, except for a few whoops and whistles. More jeers rang out, and then somebody started a chant that might have been the F-word. But that soon ended, the sounds of protest replaced by cries of dismay as the lights went out. There was still enough illumination from phones to see faces. The catcalling started again, but it was cut short.

A constellation appeared above the drummer's bowed head. Tara made out six, no, seven, points of light. The Pleiades, Tara recalled, were also known as the Seven Sisters. Coincidence? It seemed unlikely. Shining steadily with a cold and blue-white radiance, the points of light grew to orbs maybe six inches across. They drifted upstage toward the audience and then floated out above the heads of the crowd.

The youngsters had all fallen silent. Like the band, they were motionless, looking down in silence. Tara felt the power that had stilled the hundreds of people in those few seconds. Her arms felt too heavy to move and fell to her side. She bowed her head, looking at the floor illuminated by the floating orbs.

No!

Tara guessed something like this might happen. Whatever they were, the orbs had mastery over human bodies, but only at the physical level. That was her hypothesis, and it was time to test it the hard way. Tara ignored one of the orbs that moved closer and focused on her arm. Her psychokinetic power was unaffected. She'd never considered using it on herself before, but it worked fine. She raised her arm and simultaneously lifted her head.

If I'm wrong, she thought, *this could be embarrassing, if not fatal.*

She aimed the air pistol at the glowing heart of the orb and pulled the trigger from about six feet away. A pellet of pure iron found its mark, and the bright sphere dimmed and then went out.

Good; it's demonic.

The other six orbs had stopped in midair. She hoped this was a sign of confusion or preferably fear. She aimed for the nearest and fired again. This time, the pellet struck the target with a glancing blow, and the sphere wobbled but didn't vanish. The other five orbs were closing in, forming a semi-circle, but only moving at the speed of a slow walk.

Tara noticed her head and arms were not quite as heavy as before. She took another shot, and more by luck than skill, took out a second sphere. Now there were five left, and of those five, one was damaged and hanging back. The intact survivors were closing in fast now, and aiming was still tricky.

"Hey, what the hell is this?"

A girl's voice, somewhere to Tara's left. Evidently, the attackers were struggling to control everyone.

More people were recovering. Not many, maybe a dozen out of two hundred, but there was fear and confusion in the air. Someone screamed. One of the orbs broke away and swooped down at a boy with long hair and an AA tee. He tried to fend the thing off, but it changed shape the moment it touched his arm. The blue light flowed like liquid over his body. The youth froze and became a glowing statue for a moment.

Then, he was gone. At the same moment, the other orbs

vanished.

The lights came on. On the stage, Ashtaroth's Auntie looked out at the audience with slightly puzzled expressions. Then the frontman announced the next number—"Nihilist from Nashville"—to whoops of approval. Tara shoved her pistol back into her pants and looked around, trying to spot some of the people who'd woken from the trance. If anyone was troubled by what had just occurred, they didn't show it. Presumably, it was some kind of induced amnesia. Tara's psychic defenses had at least spared her that problem.

Tara left, weaving through the crowd, and pondering what to do next. Then, she remembered. She had to tell a very nice couple that she had found out what had probably happened to their daughter. They would ask the obvious question, the one Tara could only answer with promises to do more, work harder, and fight on.

Sucks to be me, she thought. *But others have it worse.*

She emerged from the old warehouse and stood for a long minute in the cool night air, relishing the drop in decibels and temperature. Then, she checked her phone. She'd received a few messages, and one was from the best-paying client she'd ever had. A man she didn't like or trust.

Tara thought of her bank balance and answered Stark's message.

CHAPTER 3

BEER, BADINAGE, AND BUSINESS

On the way to Hannigan's, Craig got a call from Tara. It wasn't a surprise. The psychokinetic freelancer had stayed in touch in the nearly three months since their first meeting at Grendon Mill.

"You on your way?" she asked.

"Yep," he replied.

It was a pleasant day, and Craig was walking across town. Being out in the sun helped counter the emotional low he'd experienced after Leroy vanished. Against that, he saw ghosts in abundance and realized he could spend the rest of his life helping them move on. How many were in this town? This county? This state? North America?

A few of the ghosts were familiar. Nellie the match girl, who was crushed to death by a runaway horse and wagon in 1873. She always hung around the same corner. Nellie looked like the archetypal waif: tiny, barefoot, her clothes in rags, and a tray of matchbooks around her neck. She had died at the age of thirteen and haunted the same neighborhood ever since.

Craig had first encountered Nellie on a cold, wet October night. Though he knew she was immune to the weather, he had still felt intense pity for the girl. But as soon as he'd revealed that he could see her, she had produced a volley of choice obscenities. Nellie did not like being seen. Craig had never gotten through to her. And here she was on her corner, apparently just mooching around, not even staring at passersby.

Keeping his distance, Craig went to the crosswalk and pushed the button.

"Yeah, just keep on walking, creep," said the now familiar high-pitched voice that was Nellie's.

Some people, he thought, *just can't be helped. Living or dead.*

He saw a few other familiar spirits as he walked the last few dozen yards to the pub. These were all mercifully pleasant or aloof. And then, he rounded the last corner and saw Hannigan's in all its slightly tacky glory. He glanced up and saw nothing but a few fluffy clouds. Sometimes, vast, strange entities drifted or circled overhead. The barrier that kept supernatural beings out of Hannigan's was catnip to all kinds of beings. Today, though, the weirder ones evidently had business elsewhere.

As he approached the door, Craig was careful to avoid contact with any of the ghosts outside Hannigan's. Not that they were dangerous as such: They simply stood outside the pub, peering into the one place they could never enter. Something was unnerving about them, or at least those who were there all the time.

Craig had a theory that being so close to the pub's mysterious shield slowly eroded a ghost. He felt it was a bit like the radioactive fallout at Chernobyl or that disaster area in Japan. The effects were trivial at first, but they soon wrought havoc unless you got away from the scene.

Despite having braved the cordon of ghosts many times, he flinched a little today.

"Craig… the seer… it is the seer…"

One of the watchers had turned from the window and seen him. Craig recognized this one. A short man in a business suit, colorless and semi-transparent. He was a gray ghost with an emaciated face and very black eyes in deep sockets. Craig wanted to help this and other watchers at some point, but communicating with them was not easy.

"Hi," he said. "I need to go inside."

Other ghosts turned now. Seven pairs of hungry eyes were on Craig. One ghost, a small woman with bobbed hair under a striking hat, moved between him and the door. She reached out a hand.

"Seer… seer… help…"

"I will," he promised, not wanting to literally walk through her. "I will, in time."

"We… need help…"

A sting of icy coldness on his shoulder made him flinch. Business Suit had laid a pale, semitransparent hand on Craig. He wriggled free and barged through the petite woman, trading one shock for another. The big front door of Hannigan's was heavy and slow to shift. In the seconds it took to get inside, he shuddered and closed his mind to the woman's memories. The gift he'd never asked for presented him with a chaos of recollections. They were, however, drained of color and emotional impact. And there was something else he couldn't quite put his finger on.

"Hey, you okay?"

A hand fell onto his shoulder, and he flinched a second time. A red-haired woman in her mid-twenties was looking at him. Behind her on a window table was a phone and a glass of beer.

"Tara! Sorry."

"No problem! I was just grabbing a drink before the meeting. Our lord and master hasn't arrived yet."

Tara gestured to the end of the bar, the one nearest the washrooms. Peregrine Stark was not in his office, which was a first. Craig was never happy in Stark's company, but somehow, the man's absence was just as disconcerting.

"He's never late," Craig said, checking his watch.

"Well, he is today," Tara said. "Get yourself a brewski, why don't you?"

Craig hesitated and then went to get a beer. Harry, the manager, was working the bar alone. Nobody knew how old Harry was, but the consensus among the regulars was that he'd served in 'Nam. The guy didn't look nearly old enough, even if he'd enlisted as a teenager at the end of the war. At a glance, Harry was a well-preserved sixty-something. Craig had never asked the guy point-blank; it was just another of the mysteries of Hannigan's. There was always the risk that if you probed such mysteries too often, they could backfire on you.

"You're early," Harry said as he poured a lite beer.

"Nah, Stark's late," Craig replied.

Harry looked mildly surprised.

"Not like him," he remarked as he set down the beer and waved away Craig's cash. "I'll put it on Mister Affable's tab. I guess you two didn't come here to socialize?"

"Right."

Back at the table, Craig had just sat when a familiar figure appeared outside the window. Peregrine Stark was not particularly tall or imposing. He was in his late forties, Craig guessed, and often unkempt, dressing like he'd just come from a thrift store. Or at least, that was the Stark Craig knew. But...

"What is it?" Tara asked, twisting in her seat to look outside. "Oh."

Stark strode in and walked to his usual place at the bar without looking around. Craig felt there was something different about the man. He couldn't put his finger on it, but Stark seemed bigger somehow. More imposing. What's more, his clothes were neater. His shoes were polished, and his jacket and pants matched.

"Color coordination; that's a first," Tara said. "I thought his schtick was to look like a random guy who's a little down on his

20

luck?"

"It was," Craig murmured. "Guess it's a different schtick now."

Stark settled on his stool and swiveled to scan the pub, his eyes resting on Craig and then Tara. Stark's face, previously round and nondescript, seemed a little thinner, and his chin was more defined. His hair was neat, too. But it was the eyes that bothered Craig. They were intense and almost predatory.

Stark smiled without a hint of warmth.

Tara sighed and stood, gathering her stuff. Craig followed her over.

"Sorry I'm late, people," Stark said. "I was unavoidably detained. But now that I'm here, let me congratulate you on your first international assignment!"

CHAPTER 4
MISSION IMPROBABLE

"Scotland?" Craig exclaimed so loudly that Harry paused in his ritual of polishing beer glasses.

"Yes. Land of the Scots," Stark said. "It's just north of England; you can't miss it. Just a few miles over the border."

Craig tried not to gawk. When Stark had asked him to get his passport processed, he thought, maybe they were going somewhere *near*, like Canada or Mexico. He'd never considered the possibility that Stark's mysterious client would want a relic from Scotland. Still, it made sense as soon as he thought about it. The world was a big place, and all kinds of weird items might be lurking in its forgotten corners.

"Where exactly in Scotland?" Tara asked. "Are we talking Berwickshire, Lothian?"

"Ah yes," Stark said, "I'd forgotten, Ms. Pride, you spent quite a spell in the UK. Did you acquire a taste for tea and crumpets?"

"Among other things," Tara said. "And you didn't answer my question, which is kind of irritating."

Stark sipped at a bottle of root beer—the only beverage Craig had ever seen him drink. He often wondered if the guy was a lightweight, or if deep down, Stark feared a loss of self-control, however slight.

"Berwickshire is spot on," he said finally. "A place called Castle McIvor. Partly ruined, and extensively rebuilt over the centuries, but a lovely place for a vacation. Beautiful countryside not far from the

North Sea. Does that suit you?"

Craig was still too nonplussed to speak. Tara sipped her beer, mimicking Stark, and then shrugged.

"I like the UK, and I like the people, but this is not a vacation," she said. "Extra trouble and risk, I'm guessing, so you'd better be upping our pay."

Craig nodded vigorously, still processing the fact that he was expected to cross the Atlantic. He made some affirmative noises as Stark haggled unconvincingly with Tara. It was obvious even to Craig that the man expected to pay more than he initially offered. And the final sum was pretty good.

"Okay. That doesn't include expenses, of course," Tara said with a sweet smile.

"Within reason," Stark said.

"Things can get kind of unreasonable with jobs of this kind," Tara pointed out. "What are we supposed to find?"

Stark leaned forward to look at Craig, who was sitting on Tara's other side.

"You're very quiet, my young friend."

Craig had to say something.

"What are we supposed to find?"

Stark reached into his jacket, took out a piece of paper, and unfolded it, flattening it on the bar. It was a photocopy from a book. It had fragments of text, but the page was dominated by an illustration that, while fairly crude, was very expressive.

"Woodcut," Tara said. "Maybe eighteenth century? Not much later, as they improved the technique so much in the 1800s."

"Perhaps," Stark said, "the subject matter is more pertinent than the technique."

Craig leaned forward. The drawing showed a castle on a hill, a rolling landscape, and another hill with a large hole dug into it. A figure in the foreground dominated the scene. A man with a huge beard wielded a sword high above his head. Around him were the mutilated remains of three men: one decapitated, and the others disemboweled. In a corner of the illustration, a woman in archaic dress was on her knees, evidently pleading for her life and those of the two children who clung to her. Judging by the swordsman's bulging eyes and snarling visage, the woman's pleas had fallen on deaf ears.

"Makes a change from a machete," Tara said. "But I guess that didn't happen on Friday the 13th at Sleepaway Camp?"

"Very astute, Ms. Pride," Stark said. "It happened in late medieval times at Castle McIvor. The story goes that the lord—more properly, the laird—of that family consulted a 'wise woman'."

Stark's air quotes emphasized the point.

"You mean a witch?" Craig asked. "Like that king in the play?"

Stark's expression became slightly more smug than usual.

"Macbeth, strictly speaking, was waylaid by the weird sisters. He didn't seek them out."

Craig, whose knowledge of classic literature was spotty at best, made a vaguely appreciative noise.

"Weird Sisters," Tara said. "Cool name for an all-girl band. Not gonna Google it. What happened? I mean, did the witch turn the laird bonkers with a curse or something?"

"Possibly," Stark said. "He was in search of gold, and she told him an ancient burial mound near the castle was a likely place to seek treasure. He ordered an excavation, and a sword was found. The laird's servants and family were promptly massacred. The alarm was raised, though, and some neighboring nobleman rode out with his retainers to see what was happening. Legend goes that the laird was brought down by a well-aimed shot from a crossbow."

"Let me guess," Tara said, "somebody picked up the sword, and the slaughter resumed."

"Indeed," Stark said. "This time, the berserk individual was dealt with promptly. Then, a Catholic priest was summoned, as the locals were convinced that the devil himself was at work. The priest picked up the sword and did not develop homicidal rage. However, he insisted that he felt a 'foul spirit' in the sword."

Stark paused and took another pull of his root beer.

"So, what did the holy man do?" Craig asked, absorbed by the tale.

"Opinions vary," Stark said. "He asked everyone to leave him alone and go out of sight, except for one mentally challenged boy who was his ward. Between them, they concealed the sword somewhere around the castle."

Tara snorted.

"Why not just break it and melt down the parts?"

Stark shrugged.

"All we can be sure of is that the sword still exists. Perhaps the priest was simply incapable of destroying it. I have good reason to believe it is in the castle or its environs. Now, who would know where it is? No living man or woman witnessed what the priest did. He took his secret to the grave. But…"

Two pairs of eyes were on Craig. He smiled nervously.

"Yeah, I get it. The local ghosts probably saw what he did. So we go and ask them and then pick up the thing that makes you into some combination of Jason Voorhees and Michael Myers."

Stark looked mildly irritated. Craig wondered if he felt popular culture was beneath him. The guy had an aura of snobbery, especially now that he was better dressed. It was another reminder that Stark and his alleged client weren't the good guys.

"Um, excuse me, but isn't there a major flaw in this plan?" Craig asked. "No way are the Brits going to let us take a sword onto a plane."

Stark waved away the objection.

"I have a trustworthy courier who will bring the sword to me by sea. All you have to do is get it and hand it over."

"You make it sound so easy," Tara remarked. "It seemed kind of straightforward last time, too. And then we ran into some serious complications."

She turned back to face Stark.

"The rival outfit, the one that sent an agent to Grendon Mill, are they after this sword?"

A shrug was the only reply.

"Not good enough," Tara said, sliding off her bar stool. "Some bitch nearly kills Craig, and you act like it's no foul? No, Mr. Stark. You can shove your magic sword where the squirrels stuff their nuts."

Craig ogled at her, confused by the imagery and surprised that she would simply turn down the job. He felt rising panic at the thought of losing some or maybe all of his income from Stark. Pissing off a guy like that had consequences. Craig had heard enough stories in this pub to be sure of that.

Tara picked up her bag, shoved her phone into her jeans, and looked at Craig.

"You coming? We make a good team; I can put some work your way."

As if it had a mind of its own, Craig's lower half started to rise from the stool. Stark, far from being furious, gave a little chuckle.

"Very well, very well, you've made your point. No need to unionize."

Tara stood with her arms folded. Craig shuffled awkwardly in place beside her. He towered over Tara, but somehow, she seemed to take up more room. Stark looked at Craig when he spoke again.

"At least one other collector is very keen to obtain the McIvor sword. There are many competent operatives in Europe, and you can expect interference. However, I believe that I have given you a head start. You are booked into Castle McIvor, which is now an upscale hotel, for fourteen days. Ample time, given your combined skills."

"Well, isn't that dandy," Tara drawled. "And we just happen to be two random tourists who love little old Scotland?"

"Not quite," Stark said with oily confidence. "You are booked in as aspiring YouTubers who also happen to be a loving young couple on a dream vacation."

Craig felt himself reddening. Tara looked at him, obviously amused.

"I hope you don't snore," she said. "Also, I call left side. And I'm a spreader."

CHAPTER 5

TERRORS, ANCIENT AND MODERN

The emaciated ghosts were gone when they left the pub. Craig sensed something overhead and avoided looking at it, keeping his eyes street-level. It was one of the ghost-eaters, and he never wanted to look at one again.

"Trouble?" Tara asked, frowning.

"Nah," he replied. "Nothing to worry about."

Tara ran Craig back to his apartment in her Land Rover. On the short journey, they discussed what had been said at the meeting and what hadn't. A thought struck Craig, a little late, as often happened.

"Why now? If this sword was hidden five-hundred-plus years ago, why bother with it today?"

Tara cursed as a cyclist shot out from a side road and into her path. Then she leaned back and expressed a familiar opinion.

"That bugger Stark has some kind of agenda, and it's time critical. He needs these things for a purpose."

"You don't think the client is real?"

"Can't rule it out, but Occam's Razor applies. And before you ask, that just means you keep the theory simple. This client is unknown and possibly nonexistent, but we know that Perry Stark is a not the most honest person. And he gave something away when we brought him the amulet. Remember?"

Craig thought back to the meeting at Hannigan's weeks ago. Upon receiving the relic, Stark had placed some tracing paper over it and rubbed the point of a crayon over a nearly invisible engraving.

This had revealed something like a seven-headed serpent or dragon.

"Did you find out what that creature was?" Craig asked.

Tara glanced at him and raised her eyebrows.

"You ever researched mythical creatures linked to the number seven? No? It's not a rabbit hole. It's a gigantic labyrinth of crazy bunnies. But one thing did tickle my interest. Gnostic gospels talk about fallen angels in serpent form. In some texts, they're called the archons."

Craig enjoyed these talks with Tara. She was like PBS in human form, always delivering nuggets of weird information. Except Tara was more fun.

"Okay, what is a Gnostic?"

"The Gnostics were a kind of network of early Christian sects who had all sorts of wild ideas. One was that our world is a kind of botched creation, a place of evil, and that only the spiritual world was truly good. It's something they had in common with the Manicheans in Persia, and they might have gotten the idea from them."

"But it says in the Bible that God created heaven and earth, and all the plants and animals. And people, of course. Adam and Eve, right?"

"Yeah," Tara said, "but remember, there's no definitive version of the Bible, only dozens of versions. Protestants and Catholics use different texts, for instance. And the original text both religions draw on was decided by a bunch of Roman bishops living hundreds of years after Christianity was founded. It's all kind of sketchy."

Craig had never discussed religion with Tara. They'd had no occasion to, but now, it occurred to him that a lot of scientists were also atheists. To him, faith, for all the problems it brought, imbued the world with a sense of purpose. He wasn't a churchgoer, but he regularly felt guilty about not going.

"You don't believe in God?" he said.

"I never said that!" Tara exclaimed. "Jeez! If you'll pardon the expression. I'm open to persuasion either way. I just pointed out that, regardless of who made the world, man made all the religions. That means a lot of ideas got dumped along the way for less-than-honest reasons. Some of the stuff the Gnostics believed might have been true, or at least half true."

"Such as?" he asked, wondering if he would get a barrage of technical terms.

"Such as the belief that the Gnostic archons—the corrupt angels that rule the Earth—were seven in number. Maybe it's a coincidence, but a couple of days ago, I encountered this demonic force that manifested as seven glowing orbs. And then, I looked for more sevens and found quite a few. Serial killers with seven victims, groups of seven involved in cult suicides. And these are all recent cases, not stuff going back decades. Maybe it's all coincidence, but it bothers me."

They had reached his apartment. There was nowhere to park, so Craig had to hop out and terminate the conversation. Tara leaned over and told him to call her that night.

"We need to have a council of war. A proper one, with Shane," she said.

"Right!" he replied, hoping he didn't sound too anxious.

He stood on the sidewalk, watching the Land Rover weave its way through the rush-hour traffic. When the car was out of sight, he went inside. Mention of Shane Ryan had brought back memories of Grendon Mill and several brushes with death. The three of them had formed a good ad-hoc team, each bringing their unique skills to the fray. But they'd had their fair share of luck. Like Shane turning up at a key moment.

The elevators were out of order again, so he plodded up the

staircase, bracing himself for ghosts. Luck was on his side in this trivial matter, it seemed. No phantoms interrupted his thoughts as he climbed four flights. No specter pounced as he made his way along the hall to his apartment.

He hesitated outside his front door. For the first time, he was not coming home to Leroy. He would never again hear that warm greeting. "How'd it go today?" It was only now that he realized Leroy had been a kind of surrogate father or kindly uncle. So what did that make Billy and Chloe?

"Big brother and little sis, I guess," he murmured, opening the door.

Billy was watching a rerun of Jeopardy! on the sofa. Chloe was nowhere to be seen. The grizzled biker didn't react when Craig closed the door.

"It's 'Who was Archduke Franz Ferdinand?', for Chrissake," Billy snarled. "What a dumbass."

A thought struck Craig as he slumped onto the sofa beside the ghost biker's hulking form. Craig had had years to study Billy's many and varied tattoos. His attention had been drawn to ones best described as NSFW. But only now did he notice that one was of a seven-headed dragon. It had faded in the years before Billy's death, so it didn't stand out too well against the tanned flesh of Billy's huge right biceps. But now that Craig looked closer, there was a resemblance to the engraving he had glimpsed before Stark had pocketed the amulet.

There was one key difference, though. The creature on Billy's arm was balancing precariously on a stylized globe of the Earth. Craig recalled a few remarks from Billy about weird guys he'd met who were into black magic and related topics.

It was worth a try. He waited until a commercial break and then asked:

"Hey, do you know anything about some old-time folks called the Gnostics?"

Billy turned his head slowly, his deep-set eyes seeming to bore into Craig.

"Yeah, but I was always more interested in medieval heretics like the Bogomils and the Cathars. Why'd you ask?"

"Well, Tara said there might be some connection with the relic we found at Grendon Mill."

Billy's big mouth twisted up in a half-smile, half-leer.

"She's not just a pretty face, huh? You could do well there, my man. Play it cool."

Craig reined in a mild rebuke and grinned inanely.

"Um, about that tattoo?" He pointed. "Is that one of the archons?"

Billy shrugged his massive shoulders, making the dragon wriggle and distorting the globe. Craig imagined cosmic powers lying in wait for humanity, and beings that could shake the whole earth for real, and felt suddenly cold.

"Guy in Sacramento did that. Year after Altamont. Yeah, that was when things turned sour. No more Summer of Love. God, that festival was such a dumb screwup! After that, bikers weren't so popular with the hippies."

Billy started cursing, his voice low and mean. Craig waited for the anger to burn itself out. He'd heard the story of Altamont, and the way the Hell's Angels had been recruited to keep order. Better than relying on The Man, the straights, and the boring respectable world of suburban rules and values. Because those suburban straights supported the war in Vietnam, so they were pretty much fascists.

Or so the Flower Children had believed until the inevitable fights broke out. And then, things had indeed turned sour. Billy had denied any wrongdoing at Altamont, and Craig gave him the benefit of the doubt. But he sometimes wondered if Billy's death had been, in part, down to a death wish. A guy didn't just take a bunch of drugs and drive into a wall at full speed in a moment of inattention.

"Sorry, little bud, you didn't need to hear that," Billy said, leaning back and closing his eyes. "Anyways, no, that's not one of the archons. Not according to the guy who inked it. It's supposed to be Yelbeghen. Different dude, maybe a cousin of the archons or something. Hard to say. Siberian monster, allegedly the son of somebody called the Golden Witch. Powerful, anyhow. A maneater. Can take the form of a dragon with seven heads or an ogre who smashes its victims to a pulp."

"Wow," Craig said. "So, is this monster supposed to be still around?"

Another massive shrug.

"Way I heard tell, Yelbeghen is buried under the snow, waiting for some kind of summons. When it comes, he'll help bring about the end of days."

"So it's a kind of Russian demon?"

"Nah," Billy said emphatically, "not Russian. We're talking about the Turks. The Turkish people are spread all over northern Asia. Turkey, the modern nation, is just one tribe. Siberia has a totally different culture from Russia."

Billy started to explain the various ethnicities of Russia's eastern provinces, but Alex Trebek reappeared and saved Craig from what might have been a long lecture. He got up and made some coffee. As he loitered by the counter, checking Wikipedia, he felt a slight breeze scented with a familiar fragrance.

Chloe was standing behind him. Whenever she appeared unexpectedly he was struck by her frailty. Huge, kohl-rimmed eyes that had seen too much dominated her small, heart-shaped face.

"You know what else is under all that snow in Siberia?" she asked.

Her expression was serious, and he thought again of a little sister earnestly telling an older sibling something momentous.

"Gold? Oil? Siberian ground squirrels?"

"Missiles," Chloe said. "Thousands of them. Primed and targeted, twenty-four seven."

"Oh, I know that," Craig said. "But it would take one incredible demon to make… I mean, it would have to… No, I can't believe it."

Chloe, having met Craig's gaze for all of ten seconds, looked down at her scuffed Doc Martens that could never be polished again.

"It's all relative, I guess. I mean, you talk to ghosts for a living, and some people wouldn't believe that," she mumbled, and then went to join Billy on the sofa.

CHAPTER 6
LOVE AND DEATH

"It's a British quest, so I thought we'd consult a British expert."

Craig couldn't dispute Tara's logic, but he was nervous. Tara was taking them to see Felicia Clovis, a woman described as 'a dealer in the same line as Stark'. That wasn't a great endorsement. Craig's experiences had taught him to be wary of people who trafficked in occult objects. They were at best eccentric. At worst they were downright psychopaths.

"Do I deduce from your silence," Tara said slowly, "that you are not one hundred per cent behind my cunning plan?"

Craig shifted in his seat and fixed his eyes on the landscape rolling by.

"I guess I'm not great at meeting new people," he said. "And yeah, that's a lame comeback. I know."

Tara shook her head.

"What went down at Grendon Mill would rattle anybody," she said. "You're doing fine. And in case you were wondering, no, Felicia can't read minds."

Craig had never even thought about telepathy. He stared at Tara, who laughed and then apologized.

"Sorry, you have that little boy lost look sometimes. It's kind of cute. Hey, we're nearly there."

A road sign loomed. They were approaching Galtonville, population 4,922. He'd never heard of the place, even though it was only a couple of hours away by winding back roads. It occurred to him that a small town like this was an odd place for any kind of business. He mentioned this to Tara.

"Oh, Felicia's one of those people who rely on rich customers to seek her out. A store in the big city would be too conspicuous—you'd get all kinds of snoopers. In a small town, it's the outsiders that are conspicuous. And she's got the locals on her side. She can be very persuasive. As in intimidating."

Craig mulled that over as they entered the outskirts of town. It was a typical mix of picturesque old-time architecture and modern decay. A Gothic-style church stood alongside a run-down pool hall that still seemed to be open for business. A boarded-up cinema showed signs of fire damage. A few pedestrians gave their car inquiring looks.

They turned off Main Street and onto Maple Drive. Here were signs of gentrification in the form of two antique stores, a small art gallery, and a fancy coffee shop. Just beyond the latter was a store with a discreet but classy façade. Shane's sedan was parked outside. Tara explained that she had called Shane the day before. He'd known of Felicia via an old friend who dealt with haunted items, and he had asked said friend for an introduction as soon as Tara mentioned they might need Felicia's expertise.

"F. Clovis, Dealer in Unusual Items," Craig read the sign up front. "Honest but nice and vague."

"I think she owns the other stores, too," Tara remarked. "Protective camouflage as well as some nice little sidelines."

Craig would have lingered to inspect the shop window, but Tara pulled him inside. The shop was surprisingly spacious. Book-laden shelves and large glass cabinets receded into shadows. The place was not well lit. There was a slight odor of incense mixed with the familiar mustiness of old books. Then Craig saw movement at the rear of the store. A skinny, seedy-looking man was discussing something with a tall, gray-haired woman in an understated business suit.

"That's her?" Craig asked quietly.

"Yeah," Tara replied.

The buyer cast a furtive glance at the newcomers, then started talking more urgently to Felicia. Craig couldn't make out what he was saying. But the British woman had a voice that carried, and he made out a word or phrase here and there.

"Careful… discreet… no refunds… advise against this…"

The skinny man waved away her protests and handed over a card. The dealer went through the rigmarole of a cashless transaction. Tara inched closer, pretending to inspect a row of jars and bottles with handwritten labels. Craig tagged along.

"Ah, there we are. It seems to take longer every time," Felica said, handing back the card. "Now, you will be careful, won't you? This kind of thing is not for amateurs."

The customer muttered something. He sounded impatient.

The tall woman produced a cardboard box from behind the counter. It was nondescript except for a dark red symbol on the lid. It was about the right size and shape for a pair of smallish shoes. The symbol was unfamiliar to Craig, but it prompted an "Oh. My. God." from Tara. The man scurried out of the shop, eyes downcast, clutching the box to his chest.

"What was it?" Craig asked as the door closed.

"There are two great motivators in life," Tara said. "Sex and money. And that guy already has plenty of money. Or at least, he did until about a minute ago."

"Really, Tara," Felicia said, emerging from behind an old-fashioned cash desk. "You think I am exploiting the weaknesses of my clientele to make excess profits?"

"No, just that particular guy," Tara shot back. "Does the poor schmuck know what he's in for?"

The tall woman shrugged.

"I can only warn and advise. An adult must take responsibility for their actions."

Craig felt like the boring guy in the bar who everybody talks over.

"What did you sell him?" he demanded.

Felicia looked at him closely for the first time.

"Ah, yes, you're the young man who keeps trying to get himself killed. Welcome!"

She gestured to a door that led into the private area of the store. As her guests followed her, she enlightened Craig.

"A succubus is a mid-range demon—essentially evil, of course—that takes the form of a voluptuous woman. This paragon of female charm is insatiable between the sheets."

"Or on the rug, or a coffee table," Tara put in. "Or atop a grand piano. Or…"

"Quite," Felicia grinned. "The experience, I'm reliably informed, is a wild ride."

Shane was standing in the back parlor, examining a vicious-looking knife with a curved blade. He looked up as Felicia entered, nodded to Tara and Craig, and then said to the dealer, "That guy bought it? Even with the warnings? Sheesh."

The dealer made a helpless gesture.

"There was a demon in the box?" Craig blurted out. "Must've been small."

The corner of Tara's mouth twitched, but she said nothing.

"No, something a little less ostentatious," Felicia explained, walking over to an antique sideboard. "It was a kit for summoning demons. An instruction manual plus various ingredients, best left unspecified. And a carefully worded disclaimer from yours truly.

Tea, anyone? Or something stronger? I have spirits and wines—even domestic beer, as well as some drinkable brands from Europe."

Craig eventually settled for tea to keep a clear head. It was Earl Grey, and the taste proved interesting, in a good way. Tara opted for a small cognac, while Shane poured himself a glass of whiskey. Felicia, teacup in hand, settled into a leather armchair opposite her guests.

"How long do you seriously think that creep will live?" Tara persisted.

The dealer shrugged.

"I don't get it," Craig confessed. "If the demon is controlled and it's really, well... you know, really..."

"Sexy as all get out," Tara put in helpfully.

"Yeah. What's the downside?" Craig asked.

Felicia leaned forward and gestured out at the shop and the wider world.

"A man having sex with a succubus knows he's doing something vile and perverted. The demon knows that he knows, and it plays on that. A word here, a facial expression there. And there are more... overtly physical ways to underline the point. It destroys its victim's self-respect."

"So why not banish it?" Craig asked.

"Because by then he's addicted," Felicia replied. "Which is why even the greatest adepts are wary of succubi. The thing drains a man physically, mentally, and spiritually."

Craig thought that over and grimaced.

"Maybe that guy wanted to die, though? He might have a terminal illness or something, and maybe thinks, well, okay, there's an upside..."

"That's some lateral thinking," Shane said. "Nobody would call it a good death. Not something I would wish on any man. Or woman."

"Woman?" Craig glanced from Felicia to Tara, who laughed.

"There's a male version of the succubus, Craig, called an incubus. And no, I never would. Not even when I'm dead drunk and buying random stuff on Amazon." Tara shook her head.

Their hostess gazed thoughtfully into her teacup.

"Sometimes it takes less than a week. Sometimes as long as a year. But sooner or later, the demon drains its victim, body and soul. By the time it abandons him, he will have lost the will to live. As a rule, they simply starve to death."

Shane chuckled mirthlessly.

"A few weeks later, a neighbor smells something funky and calls the cops."

"So why help someone die like that?" Craig protested. "I mean, okay, buyer beware, I get, but still…"

"I have refused to help people obtain a succubus dozens of times," Felicia said firmly. "But after researching his background, I made a unique exception in the case of that particular gentleman. It's far better that he expires in the arms of a succubus than carry on with his… other activities. Things that involve very vulnerable young people."

"Amen to that," Shane said dryly and set down his glass. "Okay, let's talk old swords and crazy Scottish guys."

CHAPTER 7

THE BLOODY LEGEND

Felicia produced a dog-eared tome entitled *Mysteries and Wonders of the Scottish Lowlands*. Craig immediately asked if there was anything about the Loch Ness Monster. The tall woman shook her head.

"Sadly, no. The loch is in the Highlands, you see, while our author here was writing about the area just across the border from England. So, no data on Nessie."

Craig's geography was spotty even within the USA. Tara's attempts to help with all things British had only confused him further, as she tended to give too much information.

"So... is this border a long way from London?" he asked.

"A few hundred miles," Tara said. "Not hard to get to. So, what does this particular old book have to offer?"

Felicia turned the page and pointed to a paragraph, then read aloud:

"'On that day of ill omen, the laird did take up a sword discovered in the mound. A most unnatural rage descended upon him, and he slew more than a dozen men. In his rampage, he even sought out and most foully murdered his wife and children in the very nuptial bedchamber. Since then, this room has been known as the Red Chamber. It is believed that the ghost of the laird still haunts the castle and the Red Chamber in particular, manifesting on the day of the original slaughter, the twelfth day of July. It is said that on several occasions, a man who slept in that room on the fateful day perished from no known cause. What is more, in every case, the face of the victim was contorted with mortal agony and utmost fear.'"

Craig mulled over that information.

"Is there some linking factor? I mean, were they all bad guys, or maybe psychic, or had some other thing in common?"

"I think the author would have mentioned it if that were the case," the dealer replied. "But there is a little more. 'Some men aver that these deaths are merely natural and point out that many have slept in the Red Chamber without suffering harm. However, on one occasion—according to a most reliable informant—one of the victims was obtained by body snatchers. A surgeon who purchased the corpse from these miscreants opened it to find that the heart had been cut open. The wound was of the sort that might be inflicted by a very sharp knife or scalpel, yet the skin above this fatal wound was unmarked.'"

"Now that's a neat trick," Shane commented. "And it has implications—especially for one of us."

Three pairs of eyes looked at Craig.

"Okay," he said. "In theory, I can't be killed by a ghost, but I've been hurt by plenty. And the ones at Grendon Mill were borderline cases. Unique. Maybe this Scottish one is unique in a different way. So I don't know if it could kill me. And I'm not keen to find out."

Shane grunted before Craig asked an obvious question.

"But what I don't get is this: How can a sword be haunted? I mean, we're talking Iron Age weaponry, right? And that must repel ghosts. And demons, for that matter."

"What about steel?" Tara asked. "Where do we stand on alloys and impurities?"

Felicia and Tara launched into a discussion of allotropes, molecular structure, and forging methods. When the conversation paused, Craig tentatively raised a hand, realized what he was doing, and then blushed.

"Can someone explain to me what steel actually is? I know it's a dumb question."

"Not dumb," Felicia said. "Most people don't know that steel is an alloy of iron and carbon and traces of other stuff. Stainless steel has a lot of chromium, for instance. But old-school high-carbon steel is probably what that sword was made from. A lot less likely to shatter than pure iron."

"You know, sometimes they killed a guy to harden iron," Shane added.

Seeing the effect of his words on the others, he shrugged.

"Look, this is more legend than fact, but it's been claimed that if you plunged a red-hot iron blade into a living body… well, after water, humans are mostly carbon, right?"

Tara's eyes were bright with excitement.

"Of course! That could trap a ghost in the sword. But only a seer could tell if that's the case. It might be difficult without direct contact."

Craig imagined picking up a haunted sword and found the idea unappealing. And he had another concern.

"What if it's not a ghost? What if it's a demon?"

Shane picked up the curved knife again and inspected the blade.

"What self-respecting demon would let itself get trapped in a sword and buried in a hill for a few hundred years? Or a few thousand? A weak one, maybe…"

"Or a strong one bound by even stronger magic," Tara pointed out. "We'll have to proceed with caution. But if the legend is correct, a holy man could touch it without harm. That implies there's a way to neutralize the evil. We can work on that."

Felicia, while pouring herself a second cup of tea, offered an opinion.

"Regardless of the composition of the fateful sword, a ghost or demon might theoretically inhabit the grip or hilt. Perhaps such an entity could periodically overcome its aversion to impure iron to imbue the weapon with unusual properties."

She gestured to a few other books laid out on a low table.

"Other sources offer less information, but there is one interesting sidelight on the case. The witch consulted by Laird Angus was allegedly called Mary Lennox. One writer claims that, far from telling him to dig up the mound, she'd advised Angus against it. The whole thing was his idea, not hers. Or so that particular author claims."

"She knew the sword was buried there and how dangerous it was," Craig said.

"Possibly. Or at least, she could sense some evil without knowing its precise source," the dealer said. "But, on the other hand, telling Scottish nobility not to do something might have been a good example of reverse psychology."

"If we meet the ghost of Mary Lennox, Craig can always ask her about it," Tara said. "If anyone knows where the damn thing is, it ought to be her."

Felicia smiled.

"Unfortunately, I don't have a roster of ghosts currently haunting Castle McIvor. What I do have, however, is some information on a related matter."

She stood and went to a fine old writing desk, opened a small drawer, and took out a standard business card. She handed it to Shane, who looked at both sides and then handed it to Craig without comment. At first glance, the card was unremarkable. It showed a silhouette of a man on the left side, casting a long shadow that underlined a single, unfamiliar word. FIDES.

He turned it over. There was a phone number with an international code in brackets. +44.

"Fides. I guess that's Latin," Craig said, feeling he had to say something. "And +44, if I'm not mistaken, is a UK number. So… a British outfit?"

"Correct," Felicia said. "Serious opposition with a lot of expertise. When you go to the UK, you will be on their turf."

Craig realized he'd been holding onto the card while Tara clearly wanted to see it. He handed it over. One glance was enough for her.

"The Shadow Trust."

CHAPTER 8

NOT LIKE ABBA

"Indeed," Felicia said. "The Shadow Trust might be involved."

"Never heard of it," Shane grunted. "Guessing it's big in Europe? Kind of like ABBA?"

"Not exactly, no," Felicia sighed. "The Trust has caused a lot of problems for honest collectors over the years. They tend to see every paranormal artifact or mythical site in Britain and Ireland as their personal property. And lately, they have become a lot less subtle in their approach. That's why I relocated Stateside. They kept stepping on my toes. Or I stepped on theirs. Either way, not pleasant."

Craig felt his heart sink. At Grendon Mill, a woman posing as Tara had come within seconds of shooting him dead. They had never discovered who the nameless agent was working for.

"So, who are these guys? Not a government outfit?"

"No," Tara said flatly, "but they seem to have a lot of pull with senior officials, media, politicians, *et cetera*. It didn't start out that way. The original Shadow Trust was founded in the Victorian era to promote research into the séances, hauntings, all that stuff. Searching for truth, hoping to enlighten the public, whatever. But I guess knowledge brought power and money, and they got, well, a lot shadier."

"And the 'Trust' part is a tax dodge?" Shane asked.

"Very probably," Felicia agreed. "I must emphasize that we can't be sure they are involved at all. But it's only sensible to plan for the worst. If you back off in the face of heavyweight opposition, Stark might be annoyed, of course, but—"

"Better to risk Stark's wrath than go down swinging in an unfair fight," Tara put in.

Craig reached out, and Tara handed back the card. Now that he looked more closely, there was something sinister about it. The figure casting the shadow seemed to loom threateningly. A faceless man, a nameless presence, observing but unobserved. And the word FIDES… okay, that must mean "trust". But trust in what context?

Like the Mafia, Craig thought. *'Trust me, you will regret the day you crossed me.'*

"How come you know about these guys, Tara?" Shane asked. "Did you cross paths with them in England?"

Her expression grew more serious.

"No, I didn't know anything about them until I came back to the U.S. But a few months ago, I heard that an old friend was working for them. Marcus Mortlake."

Craig recalled her discussing the British professor at Grendon Mill. In fact, he'd gotten a little tired of hearing about how brilliant Mortlake was. The guy sounded like a combination of Dr. Strange and Sherlock Holmes. At first, Craig had assumed Tara had had a crush on the professor. Then, he'd wondered if he'd been a much-needed father figure in a time of crisis. This made him feel an odd combination of guilt and jealousy that he tried to ignore. If Tara admired the man, Craig reasoned, he must be okay.

"Mortlake is a well-known researcher and an adept of no mean skill," Felicia explained to Craig. "He's only ventured Stateside a couple of times. I've had the pleasure of meeting him once or twice. He has fallen off the radar lately, though. He was last seen in Ireland under rather unusual circumstances. Oh, and he has a partner, in both senses of the term. An American archaeologist, Dr. Lynn

Carroll. It seems they have joined forces with the Trust."

The three looked at Tara, whose eyes were downcast.

"Yeah, I knew Lynn as well," she said. "We were both affected by… something dangerous. That's a chapter of my life I don't want to revisit. But I guess I might have to."

She paused and looked around at the others.

"Just not now, okay?"

Felicia got up and poured herself another cup of tea. Finally, Shane broke the silence.

"Are you concealing a serious weakness? Because if you are, it's something we should know about."

"I'm not concealing it, and nobody's invulnerable, not even the great Shane Ryan," she retorted, looking him in the eye. "But yeah, I had some bad experiences in the UK. It started with werewolves and kind of went downhill from there. I left because I wanted to put that part of my life behind me. But now, I think maybe I should confront…"

Another pause.

"Your demons," Felicia said quietly. "Inner and outer."

"Whatever it is, you're not alone," Craig said firmly. "We got the amulet as a team. That's how we'll get the sword. Demons or no demons."

Tara mouthed the word "thanks" and took a gulp of her cognac.

"This Shadow Trust," Craig said to the dealer, "is it connected to Yelbeghen?"

"I'm sure they are aware of the myth," Felicia said. "I've no reason to think it goes beyond that. While it's rightly said that everything is interconnected, that doesn't mean there's some vast conspiracy at work."

More discussion led to a consensus of sorts. Tara and Craig would follow the itinerary set out by Stark. Play it straight. Shane had other fish to fry in the next few days. They would all stay alert for interventions by other groups or individuals, especially the Shadow Trust.

"And just because you see the number seven," Felicia added, "doesn't mean it's significant. Bear that in mind the next time you pass a 7-Eleven."

CHAPTER 9
INCIDENT AT A BURGER JOINT

"I'm only helping out because I want to know what that Stark is up to," Shane said emphatically. "Not sure if that help extends to foreign travel, though. Got a lot on my plate here. And I've had my fair share of overseas service."

"I'd feel a lot safer if you were with us," Craig confessed. "Even though Stark says it should be a walk in the park."

"Huh."

Shane regarded the bite he'd taken out of his burger.

"You hear that a lot in the Corps. Guy who says it is either back at base or the first to get hit."

Tara, toying with a salad, opined that Stark was the epitome of the back-at-base optimist.

"That guy's never taken a risk in his life," she added.

Craig wasn't so sure.

"He has a lot of connections with very shady people. That card case he carries about. Details of every dubious business in the state, or maybe the country. Doesn't that mean he deals with dangerous people? Like a sleazy double-dealer in a gangster movie."

Shane took another mouthful of burger, wiped ketchup from his mouth, and responded.

"Yeah, I get that. But what if he's not a middleman? What if he's a kingpin and all those business cards just represent subcontractors to Stark Enterprises LLC?"

Tara swore.

"I don't want that to be true. I want to see him cemented into the foundations of a freeway or something. Whatever the paranormal equivalent of that is, anyhow."

Conversation languished for a while as they ate. Tara filched some of Craig's fries. He didn't notice at first as she used her telekinetic powers to slide them, one at a time, onto her plate.

"It's cute; we have to do couple stuff now!" she insisted when he protested. "We should definitely get matching outfits. Or maybe I can wear one of those 'I'm With Stupid' T-shirts."

"Hey!" Craig protested. "I think that counts as workplace bullying or something."

Shane gave an exaggerated eye roll.

"Kids today."

Craig felt an almost childish pleasure in being one of the gang, even if that meant he was the naïve one who had to have stuff explained to him all the time.

Better to belong to something than nothing, he thought. It struck him as a profound insight, but experience had taught him not to share such notions. So much time spent with lost souls had skewed his perspective.

Thoughts of ghosts took him naturally to Leroy. He took out his phone and began to delete some of the Motown tracks, but not all of them. Leroy's taste in music had rubbed off on Craig, and he kept a few of his favorites. Smokey Robinson was a no-brainer, as was Marvin Gaye.

Tara, seated next to Craig, craned her neck to check out the track listings.

"Eclectic," she remarked. "Emo shoegaze stuff, some sweet soul music, and… wow, that's a whole lot of metal. Black Sabbath! That's Ozzy Osbourne, right?"

"Right," Craig said, and explained how he played music for his support group to keep up morale. Shane, who had reduced his jumbo burger to a heap of greasy wreckage, frowned in puzzlement.

"You play them songs?"

"Why not?" Craig said. "They're human beings. Well, human souls."

Shane grunted.

"You live with ghosts, don't you?" Tara asked.

"Yeah, but they leave me alone, and I leave them alone. If I asked them what tracks they wanted for a kitchen disco, they'd think I'd gone crazy."

"Sourpuss," Tara shot back. "If I could see ghosts, I'd definitely make friends with them. The cute ones, anyhow."

The waitress returned to freshen their coffee and ask if they wanted dessert. Tara had already decided on having it as Stark was paying. Craig felt he had room for a little more. Shane was impatient to be getting home, though, and left some cash before bidding them farewell.

"You think he'll join us?" Craig asked.

He had a sudden flashback to Grendon Mill and the way Shane had appeared in the nick of time. It would be preferable to have the guy with them, bringing all his experience to bear, from the start.

"We've got a week 'til our flight," Tara pointed out. "I'll persuade him. He's one of those guys who prefers to work alone. They're an asset in a lot of situations: self-reliant, adaptable, strongly motivated. But sometimes, you need team effort. Whatever Stark is up to…"

She paused as two large desserts came into view. Craig had opted for cheesecake, and Tara for peach cobbler. The discussion was paused for a couple of minutes, except when Tara tried to filch some of Craig's dessert. This time, however, she had to use the standard method of swiftly attacking with a spoon, and he parried the thrust.

Then Shane reappeared, looking pissed.

"Problem?" Craig asked.

"Yeah, you could say that. Someone stole my car."

CHAPTER 10

FISH IN A BARREL

"See?" Shane said. "I parked my car where I could see it, but this guy decided to park right next to it."

It was true. Shane's sedan had been obscured by a high-sided truck. Tara's Discovery, by contrast, was in plain sight from inside the restaurant.

"We could be questioning ghosts," Craig said, looking around the parking lot. "You might have a non-living witness to the crime."

Craig and Shane spread out, going to opposite ends of the lot. Craig hoped to see an obvious ghost, one that loitered here permanently. But none of the handful of people around stood out. Craig looked twice at a woman pushing a little boy in a stroller. She was pale-faced and anxious, moving as if in a dream. They proved to be alive when the mom maneuvered her fractious toddler into a huge SUV. That slightly spectral look was probably due to a lack of sleep.

To their credit, the county police arrived just ten minutes after they called 911. One of the officers expressed incredulity when Shane described his car but quickly fell silent at the resulting glare. The other cop, a woman older than her colleague, was sympathetic and efficient.

"We can pull the security camera footage," she said, "but now that we've got the license plate number and description, finding your pride and joy might just be a matter of waiting."

The cops left, having provided a contact number and more

encouragement.

"You going to get a rental?" Craig asked.

"Guess I'll have to. I need to get to a few places from here. An Uber won't cut it."

"We'll take you to the nearest agency." Tara was already searching on her phone. "Oh, maybe twenty minutes. Let's say half an hour with traffic. Maybe we can even somehow finagle the cost out of Stark."

Two minutes later, Tara was negotiating the late-afternoon traffic.

"Think we got a tail," she said, twisting around to look past Craig and out the back window. Craig turned to see a black van with tinted windows very close behind.

A sudden chill started goosebumps on Craig's arms. The air conditioning was on, but it seemed like the temperature in the car had dropped by several degrees.

"Hey…"

Someone was crouching between Tara and Shane. Craig could make out the road ahead through it. Shane was already moving, but in the confined space, he had to lean back awkwardly to direct a blow. This gave the intruder a second, and it seized the opportunity. The ghost vanished just as Shane's fist lashed out, narrowly missing Tara.

"Sorry," Shane said. "I'll be quicker if he…"

Tara was hunched forward far more now, and Craig could see her face in the rear-view mirror. Her expression was manic, her mouth twisted into an evil grin, and her eyes wide and staring. The SUV accelerated sharply, throwing Craig back into his seat.

"What the—?"

Shane reached to grab the steering wheel. Tara was swinging the Discovery left, toward the central barrier of the highway.

Screeching brakes and blaring horns made a cacophony as Shane gripped the wheel with both hands.

Craig unbuckled his seatbelt and lunged forward just as they narrowly missed a Toyota. Craig hit his head on Tara's seat and fell sideways. He got a glimpse of a child in the front of the other car, his mouth open in terror. Craig's second try got him in contact with Tara, his hand on her right shoulder.

He sensed the ghost at once. It was sly and strong, used to this kind of attack, joyfully anticipating the wreckage of this car and, with luck, a few others, too. Craig recoiled from the amoral cruelty in the spirit, but then rallied and focused his attention.

"You can move on!" he shouted.

It had the desired effect. The ghost was distracted, losing its grip on Tara, who Craig sensed had been struggling all along. The brief window of opportunity was past. The ghost slipped away, out of Craig's field of perception, and Tara was okay. Craig let go of her shoulder.

"It's gone. For now, at least."

"We need to stop before they try—"

Shane didn't finish his thought. Another ghost appeared beside Craig. It was a woman, thin-faced and pale, with a vicious mouth. Before he could react, she had plunged red-nailed fingers into his chest, and he felt her icy grip on his heart. He thrashed around, weaponless. Then, the cruel grasp was gone, the phantom's power spent. Craig couldn't be killed by a ghost. Unfortunately, malign ghosts were usually unaware of this. They often inflicted a lot of pain until they ran out of juice. Shane was looking back at him anxiously.

The black van had fallen behind out of sight, but they soon discovered that was irrelevant. A third ghost appeared on the hood of the SUV. It was a little girl with her ginger hair in pigtails, her clothes suggesting she'd died in the Forties or Fifties. Compared to the earlier attacker, she seemed almost comical, until she launched herself through the windshield at Tara.

Shane was ready for her, but not for the other ghost that dropped through the roof. The front seats became a roiling chaos of limbs, opaque and transparent, as the living fended off the malevolent dead. But Craig was armed now. Tara's sports bag was on the back seat, and he'd pulled out iron knuckledusters. It was impossible to strike without hitting his companions, but he pulled his punches just enough.

The second attacker fled into nothingness, but the little girl was a tougher target. One moment, her limbs wrapped around Shane, and then somehow, she'd dodged into the footwell while laughing frenziedly. Every time Shane aimed a blow at the girl, she vanished and then reappeared to grab his arm. Craig opened a vial and threw it. Iron filings filled the footwell, and the girl disappeared.

No more attacks came. Tara took the next exit and, after driving a few hundred yards, found a Walmart. Craig realized that his heart was pounding. Sweat had pooled unpleasantly at his crotch and dripped down his torso from his armpits. He did not feel even slightly heroic, but Shane gave him a thumbs-up sign.

"Quick thinking. Well done."

They got out and spent a few moments taking in the scene. Homemakers pushed shopping carts, fuel-efficient mid-range cars arrived or departed, and a couple of kids screamed at each other while their mom talked on her phone. Craig checked, but as far as he could tell, everyone he saw was alive.

"I'm sorry," Tara said finally. "I'll do better. I swear I will do better."

She couldn't meet either man's eyes. Craig put an arm around his colleague.

"They got the jump on you once; it won't happen again."

Tara still didn't look up.

"Thing is, it's happened before. I thought I'd worked on my defenses. Put up barriers."

Shane looked her in the eye.

"No such thing as a perfect defense, Tara. We do our best to prepare but also be ready to improvise."

Her "thanks" was barely audible. She squeezed Craig's arm and gently broke free.

"So, what now?" Craig asked.

Shane looked back at the way they came.

"I don't know about you, but I'm going to get my goddamn car back."

CHAPTER 11

NIGHTMARE AT 30,000 FEET

Craig had never enjoyed airports, but his time at Logan International was unusually difficult. He kept thinking about the attack on the highway and wondered if it would occur again. In theory, a ghost could simply stop a person's heart, give them a cerebral hemorrhage, or kill them in any of a dozen other ways. It might raise eyebrows if Craig and Tara died simultaneously of an obscure cause in a public place, but if somebody wanted them dead, a brief flurry of media interest might be a price worth paying.

After the usual holdups, confusion, and security theater, they finally embarked on their flight to London. It was on time, the airline staff was friendly, and the general atmosphere was calm, just as one might expect. But Craig couldn't help scrutinizing his fellow passengers for suspect behavior or even shifty expressions.

"Stop staring at people," Tara hissed as they made their way toward their plane. "They'll think you're a terrorist or something. You look weird."

They found their seats, put their carry-ons in the overhead compartment, and settled down. Tara had the window seat; Craig was in the middle. To his right was a young American who introduced himself as Zack. He said a polite hello and explained that he was a grad student on his way back to the UK after a visit home. Soon, he and Tara were exchanging anecdotes about British life. Craig asked about the weirdest thing he should expect.

"No light switches in the bathrooms," Tara said. "They're

outside the door, or you have to pull on a cord that works a switch in the ceiling."

"That is kind of strange," Zack agreed, smiling. "But what about all those accents? If you travel an hour from London, it's like a different language. They have so many words for, like, a bun, and it's such a small country!"

The conversation went back and forth for a while, then Zack announced he was kind of pooped and needed some sleep. He was soon dozing, his earbuds in place.

"Not a bad idea," Tara remarked, and followed suit. "Get some shuteye, Craig. Jet lag can be a bitch."

Craig couldn't close his eyes. He tried to watch the in-flight movie, but he couldn't concentrate. Even a love triangle involving Sandra Bullock couldn't stop him thinking about the attack they'd survived only a week ago. It seemed obvious that smuggling a ghost onto a plane was far easier than concealing a regular weapon.

Sure, ghosts couldn't kill him by direct assault, but what if a ghost killed the pilots and started monkeying with the flight controls? How could he avert that kind of indirect attack?

Something else bothered him, too. Something Zack had said was worrying at the back of his mind, making him fretful and anxious above and beyond his aversion to flying.

"Stop fretting over things you can't control," Tara had told him more than once. "It'll be fine."

Craig smiled weakly and had to agree that he was being paranoid. Nothing had happened beyond the usual hassles every airport specialized in. He dozed fitfully, snapping awake once when Zack got up to use the toilet. He was awoken a second time for the in-flight meal of generic chicken. After that, he dozed again, and when he next checked their position, they were nearing the so-called point of no return, where it became impossible for the plane to head back to the U.S. Any problems now, and they would have to press on toward London or maybe divert to Iceland? Craig was vague on such matters and wished he'd checked beforehand.

Stop being silly, he told himself. *Flying is perfectly safe. Well, not perfectly, but...*

He glanced over at Tara. It seemed that she had been asleep for hours. Flying long-distance held no worries for her. He looked past her, out of the tiny window. Darkness was falling on the Atlantic. The setting sun was not visible, but the sunset was painting the sea and sky in splendid purples and reds. Their seats were just right by the wing, so his view was partly blocked.

Craig was about to lean back and close his eyes when something fluttered up from below. For a second, he thought it might be a floater inside his eyeball, but then it passed out of sight before reappearing. Could it be a high-flying bird? He dismissed the idea as ridiculous. No bird could fly this high, and besides, the thing in question was nebulous, its outline vague. A cloud of smoke? No, they would leave smoke far behind in an instant. Whatever it was, it kept pace with the airliner. And now, it clung to the leading edge of the wing and then began to move along it, oozing like an amoeba.

"Tara!" he hissed urgently.

She moaned softly and turned her head away from him. Craig jabbed a finger into her biceps. He had lost sight of the mysterious blur. Then, he saw it again, sliding or oozing off the wing and down onto the engine mounting.

"Tara, wake up!" he said aloud.

"Carl! No!" she said and then woke up.

Startled, they stared at one another. Craig didn't have time to ask who Carl was but pointed out into the twilight.

"Something is out there!"

Tara frowned, twisted around, and leaned close to the window, blocking Craig's view. Then, she leaned back and shook her head.

"You must have had a bad dream, Craig."

He stared out at the wing, the engine, and the darkening sky. A bright star, Venus perhaps, was visible now. Had he imagined the flickering shape? Optical illusions occurred in unusual conditions, and he was on edge. He peered out of the window for another few moments and then leaned back. A loud laugh from another passenger prompted him to turn his head, and he found himself looking at Zack. The student's eyes were closed and his lips were moving. He had taken out his earbuds, and his fists were clenched, the knuckles white. Was the young American praying?

"Are you okay?" Craig asked.

Zack's eyes opened, and a second later he smiled in a goofy, lopsided way.

"Yeah, sure. I just got this mantra I repeat sometimes. Helps me focus, you know?"

"Sounds cool," Craig said, and looked back at the TV screen on the seat back before him.

For the briefest instant, before Zack had smiled, he had seen something in the guy's face. A seriousness that seemed out of character. Or perhaps a glimpse of the stranger's true nature?

The rest of the flight to London was uneventful, but Craig didn't sleep at all.

CHAPTER 12

MOST HAUNTED

Heathrow. The name had a quaint, rural feel to it, conjuring images of meadows and quaint English cottages, but Craig knew better. He had read many online comments about London's biggest airport. Everyone agreed that it was terrible, so he wasn't too shocked by the noise and general chaos. It seemed like people from every nation were passing through, and a very large percentage were being parted from their baggage in the process. Also, the place looked half-finished, as he remarked to Tara.

"Yeah, it's always like that," she said, making an exaggerated grumpy face. "They keep trying to build an extra terminal and stuff, but politicians dither, and the local people object. Boris Johnson used to be the member of parliament for the area, and he promised both sides that he'd do what they wanted. It's just a goddam mess."

"And 'terminal' is a hell of a word to use," Craig remarked. "I mean, as if the whole setup isn't bleak enough. Couldn't they call it something else? Like a plane pier, or maybe a sky jetty?"

Tara's previous time in England came in handy as she ushered Craig through the various bureaucratic hurdles. They recovered their luggage intact and eventually got outside, where drizzle fell from clouds of gunmetal gray. Tara held out a hand as if to catch some drops and smiled perkily.

"British summer. Enjoy!"

"Yay!" Craig responded, forcing a smile.

Tara had booked a cab that took them to a mid-range hotel. The price of the short ride was eye-watering. As they were posing as YouTubers, Tara took footage on her phone and kept up a running commentary. It was surprising how positive she could be, given how dreary their prospect was.

The area around the airport was bland and didn't give Craig much sense of being overseas, but here and there, he saw signs of a different culture. Actual signs, in the case of the road, with names that might have come out of a Harry Potter novel. Feltham. Staines. West Bedfont. When he caught sight of a McDonalds followed closely by a Starbucks, he felt a little homesick but also reassured.

"Yeah," Tara commented, seeing where he was looking, "the Brits love fast food. And also slow food like a Sunday roast or a full English breakfast. And that's before they get stuck into world cuisines. You shouldn't believe what people say about the food here, by the way. You can get pretty much any kind of meal in London, from burgers to tacos and Indian or Thai."

Their hotel was fine in a newly built, soulless way. The cost, again, struck Craig as almost extortionate. He was glad Stark was paying. To maintain their cover story, they had a double room with separate beds. A kettle, mugs, and various sachets stood on a side table. Tara recorded some more footage of herself making a cup of tea, chattering brightly to Craig as if they'd been partners for years. He didn't feel comfortable about being filmed, but they'd agreed to take their roles seriously.

"I guess you'll want coffee, sugar?" Tara asked.

"Um, yeah," he said, returning her smile. "Not sure if I'll ever be a tea person."

Tara held out the phone to capture them.

"Well, maybe you'll change your mind when I introduce you to the pleasures of dunking."

"Dunking? That sounds... a little kinky."

She punched him lightly on the upper arm.

"Naughty! This is a family-friendly channel! We don't want to get demonetized, do we?"

Tara stopped filming.

"I got a good reaction from you there," she remarked, dipping a teabag into a mug of steaming tea. "When I splice it together, that'll make our fifth upload."

Craig, who'd been stirring sugar into his coffee, paused in surprise.

"You already made some videos?"

Tara explained that their YouTube channel had been set up by Stark a few weeks earlier. It contained some generic videos of the haunted house variety with commentary by Tara but nobody on screen. The same went for their presence on Instagram and Facebook. There were pictures of Tara and Craig, and links to Craig's ghost tour side hustle. There were comments from various users, some of them seemingly from hardcore followers. These were, of course, fake accounts. It was not the kind of cover that would stand much scrutiny, but it would satisfy most people.

"The point is to have a reason to ask about ghosts," she reminded him. "I'll act the part of the loud American who just loves everything they clap eyes on, and you can be the quiet one. Double act. Like Abbott and Costello, only in real danger."

Craig sometimes found Tara's references confusing, but he'd seen a few Abbott and Costello movies. Soon, they were talking about comedy shows and related topics like actual friends. Sitting on the bed while Tara lolled on a small couch, Craig found himself wondering about her. She knew what he was, the powers he possessed, and the burdens he carried. She, too, had had to come to terms with her wild talent of psychokinesis. She had hinted at dark times. Might they become an actual couple?

The conversation lagged, and Craig suppressed a yawn.

"Well," Tara said, "guess we'd better get some shuteye!"

As she spoke, she leaned forward and slapped her knees with the palms of her hands. Seeing his confusion, she chuckled and repeated the knee slap.

"Oh, see, this is how a Brit ends a conversation. Or leaves a party, or goes home after dinner at your place. You never say, 'I'm going'; there's always a ritual. You'll get used to it. Maybe try it out sometime!"

They spent the next few minutes in slightly awkward preparations for bed. Craig fished out the adapter to charge his phone and waited while Tara used the tiny bathroom. The sound of her showering inevitably led to thoughts of her naked. Craig wondered if she had scars from the various encounters with demons, werewolves, and other entities. He felt furtive and slightly ashamed, but also excited. He was taking a fake holiday with an attractive woman as part of a covert mission. Shouldn't he be feeling more like a cool, talented guy and less like a perv?

"All yours," Tara said, emerging in a hotel bathrobe. "And watch out for that towel rail, I think it's somehow tapping heat from the Earth's core."

"Right," he mumbled, edging past her.

Craig decided to shower the next morning and just washed his face before brushing his teeth. The bathroom mirror was steamed up, and he wiped it to check his appearance. He looked worn out, which was not surprising. Craig couldn't remember how many time zones he'd crossed that day, but he felt as if each one had taken years off of his life. He thought back to the plane and to Zack the student. Again, he worried that he'd missed something crucial, that a key fact had eluded him.

"Ah, screw it. Get some sleep."

He yawned again, stretching his cramped muscles with his eyes half-closed. At that moment, something moved in the mirror. A vague shape loomed behind him, absorbing the light. The bathroom was suddenly in shadow, and Craig spun around, his panic rising. Nothing was there, no towering figure formed from darkness.

"You okay in there?" Tara called.

He must have cried out.

"Yeah, I think so," he replied, opening the door. "It might have been my imagination. But it might have been a ghost, just there for a second."

Tara was lying on the bed, encased in an oversized T-shirt bearing the slogan GHOSTVLOGGERS DO IT IN STREAMS. It was one of several items designed to make their cover story seem credible. Craig suspected it would merely make them look stupid, but he was prepared to play along. Her legs and feet were bare and, so far as Craig could see, unscarred by past battles. He tried not to stare at her toes, their nails painted alternately in red and white. She laid down her phone and smiled at him.

"I guess you're going to see a lot of ghosts. They say this is the most haunted country on Earth."

Craig had not given much thought to how common or distracting British ghosts might be. He decided to tackle the problem if it arose and change the subject.

"Did you have any luck? With Marcus?"

He gestured to her phone, and her expression became serious.

"His old number's defunct, along with his emails, work and personal. St. Ananias College claims he's on an extended sabbatical, which is BS, but I guess all the proper procedures have been followed."

He sat on the edge of his bed. As an expert on all things paranormal in the UK, Marcus Mortlake would be a powerful ally.

But if he was working for the Shadow Trust, he might thwart their plans. Tara insisted he'd never do something outright immoral; never hurt her or anyone she was with. Craig wanted to believe her, but he'd lost count of the ghosts he'd met who, while being spotless characters in life, admitted to appalling conduct when questioned after death.

"Still," he said, trying to lift her mood, "we've got Shane on our side. Assuming he gets his car back."

Tara seemed to cheer at the thought.

"Yeah, I'd hate to be the clown who stole that car. Shane seems to be your classic 'don't touch my stuff' type."

They doused the lights. Craig undressed in the dark and slid under the covers. As soon as his head hit the pillow, he sank into a deep slumber. When he woke, unsure of the time, he saw Tara's face illuminated by her phone, her expression serious. He almost spoke but decided to leave her. If she was having trouble sleeping, starting a conversation would not help.

He was about to turn over when a figure appeared, standing over Tara. It was tall, and dressed in black, with a pale, emaciated face. A wide mouth grimaced at the unsuspecting woman.

CHAPTER 13

STRANGERS IN THE NIGHT

Craig leaped out of bed and shouted a warning, fumbling with the light switch. Tara got out of her bed to stand by him, her eyes wide. They had no weapons to use against ghosts, at least not technically, but they had smuggled a couple of small items through airport security. Tara had worn a large brooch, which she'd put alongside her phone and keys when going through the metal detector. It was iron, including the large pin. Now, she picked it up from the bedside table. Craig seized his belt, which had a cast-iron buckle.

The ghost's mouth opened, revealing gap teeth, most of them brownish stumps.

"He still in the same place?" Tara asked.

"Yeah. Direct line from you to the couch," Craig whispered.

Tara tossed the brooch into the air. It arced toward the bed, falling far short of the intruder. Then her power kicked in, and the brooch hurtled straight at the ghost, moving far too fast to dodge. It didn't strike the phantom squarely, but for a shot at an unseen target, it was pretty good. The brooch went straight through the ghost's right shoulder before hitting the wall with a loud clack. The spirit disappeared, but reappeared after a few minutes later, about eighteen inches to the left of where it had been.

Craig was giving a fast commentary. The brooch lifted in the air and started to whirl outward in a spiral, the growing arcs bound to intersect anything on that side of the small room. Craig, meanwhile, started to edge around the bed, swinging the belt, ready to lash out.

"No! No, stop, I pray you!"

The ghost raised two slender white hands in supplication, at the same time falling to its knees. It was begging for mercy, and Craig asked Tara to hold back. The brooch faltered in midair and then fell to the carpet. Craig knew Tara's power was physically and mentally draining. She would probably be exhausted 'til the next day. Too much exertion, and she might pass out. Even if the ghost was using a ploy to buy time, letting the psychokinetic recover made sense.

"Why are you here?" Craig demanded.

Now that he had time to study the interloper, Craig saw that the ghost was almost certainly male and dressed in very archaic clothes. A dark brown cloak with a hood thrown back partly covered faded garments of a greenish color. A gold shoe buckle was just visible, peeking out from under the flowing cloak. The costume fitted with the archaic phrase, "I pray you!" It was a figure from centuries ago. The ghost's face, framed in long, lank hair, was not malicious but melancholic. Whatever had kept this spirit from moving on must, Craig felt, have been tragic. He'd seen many such ghosts, lost and lonely, but never one so ancient. A creature to inspire pity.

"I am but a messenger, my good lord."

The ghost's English was comprehensible, but the accent was odd. Not exactly posh British, but something like it. Craig repeated the sentence word for word to Tara and then demanded to know the message.

"Do not seek the sword!"

Craig's spirits fell. It was just a dumb warning after all. When he passed that on to Tara, she sneered in the general direction of their guest.

"Oh, sure. We flew three thousand goddamn miles just to turn around and go home? Give me a friggin' break."

The ghost turned his melancholy face toward her and then

looked back at Craig.

"That one has shed the blood of the guilty, but she has also taken the life of the innocent," he whispered urgently. "She has been used by monsters and might become one. Do not trust her!"

Craig shouted an obscenity to blot out the last of the warning. He was angry because of the insult to Tara, but also because the ghost's tactic was so obvious. Divide and conquer, sow suspicion, and undermine trust in a strong team. He advanced, swinging the belt, longing to send the iron buckle through the bloodless features.

"What is it?" Tara asked.

The iron brooch wobbled upward, not moving so fast or certainly this time. Jet lag had probably taken its toll on her power. The ghost retreated, a supplicant once more, its hands clasped in prayer.

"It's telling lies," Craig said, "to make me mistrust you."

The brooch circled behind the ghost and shot through its abdomen, causing him to disappear once more. Craig relaxed and slumped onto the bed. His heart was racing. Tara sat beside him and took his arm in her hands.

"You did good, partner! What did it say?"

Seeing him hesitate, she grew more serious.

"Hey, no secrets, right? We're a team. I can take it."

He repeated what the ghost had said and Tara looked down, her disheveled hair falling over her eyes. She had never looked so beautiful. His heartbeat had not slowed.

"I see," she said quietly. "I guess I owe you an explanation for that. I should have told you straight off. In Grendon Mill or at least straight after that. But I guess... well, it's not something to brag about."

They sat for nearly an hour, Craig in silence, his eyelids heavy. She talked in disjointed phrases at first as she struggled to find a way into the story. Then, she started again, matter-of-factly with no regret and no words of self-justification. Now and again, he had a strange sensation that he was listening to a stranger, someone mimicking the voice of Tara Pride. Someone younger and far more fragile.

She talked of the werewolf attack that had slain her boyfriend, and the way her search for the truth had taken her to Marcus Mortlake's door. She told him about a haunted house in the north and the way a demon lurked beneath it, harvesting the souls of the dead. And she revealed how her power to move matter had been triggered by the entity, killing an innocent stranger and almost ending the life of a good friend.

"Fire?" he said. "You... you burned a guy?"

"No, no, I didn't!" she insisted plaintively. "The demon, god, whatever you call it, took possession of me and used a power I didn't even know I had. It was part of a supernatural game, you see? No, of course, you don't. It's crazy. I've written it down and told people I trusted: my brother, my best friend from college, and someone I thought I could build a life with. But none of them believed me. I wouldn't believe it either if I hadn't lived it. It defies logic, common sense, and everyday experience. I was possessed. More than once. And more people got hurt."

She raised her eyes to his. She was crying silently, with no hint of sobs or gasps. A second later, he was hugging her and saying anything that might make things better. He talked about his loneliness and fears, the despair he felt in the past about sharing the world of the dead, and feeling like a stranger among the living. He tried to let her go after a while, disengaging slowly and gently, but she put her arms around him and pressed her head against his chest. Saying nothing more, they sat like that until he heard her breathing with the regular, placid rhythm of sleep. Then he laid her down, covered her, and put out the light. He lay beside her until morning.

Craig did not know when he fell asleep, only that when he woke, he was under the duvet, and Tara was gone. A note on the pillow explained that she would see him downstairs for breakfast, followed by a winking emoji. Underneath, she had drawn three small hearts.

CHAPTER 14
FULL ENGLISH BREAKFAST

Craig's plate was heaped with protein, carbs, and fat, cunningly disguised as baked beans, two sausages, a fried egg, some mushrooms, and hash browns. He poked at the latter with his fork.

"Are hash browns traditional over here?"

"They are now," Tara said, leaning back in her chair and surveying Craig's breakfast. "I heard they were introduced in the nineties. Kind of a standard hotel thing. Easy to prepare. Most Brits don't eat them, though."

Craig gave a "huh" of mild interest and cut into a "banger", as the sausages were known for some reason. He swirled the segment of pinkish meat around in the tomato sauce and wolfed it down. It tasted good to a hungry man. He'd not eaten much on the plane, and last night had been draining. He noticed that the remnants of Tara's breakfast suggested she felt the same. She'd had quite a feast.

Tara leaned forward and Craig followed suit. It was evidently time to talk shop.

"Maybe I'd better go alone to see Stark's guy."

Craig was puzzled. They'd not discussed the details of who would do what, but he'd assumed they'd be together. They'd made an effective team in Grendon Mill after some initial hiccups. Seeing his expression, Tara reached out and touched his hand. He felt his face reddening a little and looked down at his plate.

"What I mean is, this meeting is in the middle of London," she explained. "We're on the outskirts here, but Camden is bound to be chockful of ghosts. It might be kind of overwhelming."

Craig had given this some thought. London, he knew, was more than two thousand years old. It had been the world's biggest city in the Victorian era. Of course, it would be replete with the unquiet dead. Most would be merely lost souls and no trouble to anyone; the ghosts that passed close to an oblivious mortal on a warm summer's day. Such a ghost would often give a living person a sudden, inexplicable chill, accompanied by a feeling of despair or loneliness.

But there was a percentage of malicious or mischievous ghosts in any city and how Craig reacted to them in an unfamiliar, crowded metropolis might be problematic. As he mulled it over, he could see how Tara might worry about him. But there was another factor to consider.

"What if there's another attack?" he asked. "If I'm not there to see it coming, you might not be able to react in time."

Tara smiled ruefully and munched a last morsel of buttered toast. Craig guessed she was thinking of the vulnerability she had shown a few hours ago. She shrugged.

"There's no ideal way to do it, I guess, especially without Shane. I guess I'm a little overconfident because I used to live in London. All big cities are dangerous places, especially if you're on your own. You're right; we'll go together."

Craig ate steadily while Tara went over the inventory of equipment Stark's contact should have. Falling foul of British laws before they even reached their objective would be embarrassing. They didn't want guns, but there were strict regulations on knives and other weapons, too. The ways around them were fairly ingenious, Craig had to admit. But then, most things their employer did reeked of duplicity and deception.

Craig stood up to get more toast.

"Need a refill?" he asked, pointing at Tara's coffee cup.

"Nah, I'm good."

He walked over to a table where a machine with a conveyor toasted bread. He was always slightly daunted by such contraptions but had more or less figured this one out. Just as he picked up two slices of bread, however, someone cut in ahead of him. The man looked like a businessman, slim and stoop-shouldered, wearing a dark suit. His hair was very black and disarrayed.

Craig wasn't sure about the etiquette in this situation. He settled on saying, "Oh," in a slightly disapproving tone. The other man didn't react. In fact, he didn't do anything, just stood there with his back to Craig. Craig cleared his throat. Nothing.

"Excuse me, sir, um, is there a problem?"

The man straightened up. Craig set down his bread on a nearby plate and prepared for a tricky dialogue. He'd been slow to grasp the situation. People died in hotels, and a few would be condemned to haunt them. In the time it took for the stranger to turn around, Craig visualized an overworked salesman clutching his chest and pitching forward. Maybe the poor man had face-planted into his full English breakfast, the last of many that had helped him along the road to a coronary. And now, he was doomed to haunt the characterless dining room of a London hotel.

The suited man looked up at Craig and smiled apologetically. The guy was Asian, maybe Chinese, with glasses, and a round, amiable face. He gestured at the toast machine and then at Craig, and spoke a few hesitant words.

"You know... toast... how I work this?"

Craig thought this was a terrible fate. Destined to want toast indefinitely and never get it. But then, the stranger shoved a plate with two slices of brown bread on it in Craig's direction. Craig took the plate instinctively. This was no ghost.

Craig stared and then laughed in relief.

"Oh, sure! No worries."

He gave a little demonstration and was thanked profusely in two languages. Walking back to their table, he saw Tara grinning. Of course, she'd watched the little drama.

"This is the Nth time I've done that on a mission," he said with a grimace. "Need to work on my ghost determining skills, or whatever."

"It's natural," she replied. "Unfamiliar surroundings put us on our guard. We're disposed to see threats where there are none and miss the ones that are there. And you did your good deed for the day like a regular Boy Scout. A man got his toast, and all's well with the world. Now finish up; we've got an appointment at Camden Market."

They got a cab to the nearest London Underground station. On the Tube train, Craig saw a taste of home: a lot of people staring at their phones and resolutely not making conversation. He mentioned this to Tara, who said that the farther you got from London, the friendlier the people were.

"Figures," he said.

The temperature in the Tube car was hot, not quite uncomfortable but getting there. Craig found himself nodding off. Tara nudged him upright when he slumped against her.

"Sorry, still jet-lagged," he mumbled.

The first time it happened, Craig barely noticed. The car was getting crowded, and the ghost flashed by in a blur like a shadow moving swiftly. But Craig was ready the second time and got a better look. He still only saw a face with its mouth open and its eyes wide. The body was cut off by the floor of the car. The Tube train braked, and the next ghost moved slowly enough for Craig to make out archaic clothes, gray hairs, and a lined face.

"Did a lot of people die building this tunnel?" he asked Tara.

"Maybe. Why do you… oh," she said. "Maybe the Tube wasn't a good idea."

Craig dismissed it.

"I can't go through life wrapped in cotton wool. Unless I live like a hermit in the middle of the desert, I'm going to see ghosts. The living are always accompanied by the dead."

Craig didn't feel as stoical as he sounded. He had guessed what might be awaiting him at Camden Town Station. He'd ridden the New York Subway once, and it was haunted by some of the most tormented specters he'd ever seen. London's Underground was older than the subway, so it was likely to have more ghostly inhabitants.

The train braked again, and people got up and clustered near the doors. He followed Tara and joined the ragged queue, hanging onto a strap that dangled from the roof of the car. The train lurched, throwing Tara against him. The distraction meant he almost missed the ghost as it plunged off the platform and under the train. Or almost under. Part of it was still visible for a few moments. The bloody limb that could have been a leg or an arm had been messily severed.

The ghost was one of the saddest variety, condemned to repeat its death for decades or even centuries until it faded away. Craig wondered if he could do something for it. As they got off the train, he took Tara's arm and led her aside. When he explained what he wanted to do, she looked around at the crowded platform. Now that the passengers who had disembarked were gone, the place was almost deserted, but people were arriving by the second.

"It will draw some attention, but if you want to…"

"I'd like to," he said, looking over her head to the place where the ghost waited.

Craig could make out an advertisement through the ghost.

Semitransparency was sometimes down to a ghost seeking to be unnoticed by seers like Craig. But he could end their suffering now.

Tara walked alongside him and kept up some inane chatter about her years in London to provide some cover for Craig's conversation. As he got closer, he saw that the ghost was a young woman, maybe in her late teens or early twenties. She had light brown skin, bobbed black hair, and a pink tote bag marked Happy Times.

"Hello," he said quietly. "I can see you."

The ghost turned, and he saw her face for the first time. It was almost expressionless and quite serene. He had seen this in suicides before, and it always upset him. The period of despair and suffering had ended with the decision to end a life that seemed unlivable. The ghosts always spoke of the elation they felt and a sense that all burdens had been lifted. No more struggle, no more bullying, and no more failure. A loveless, futile existence ended. It was a strange liberation, but it cast its spell on millions every day.

"Leave me alone," the girl said.

Using guesswork, Tara positioned herself on the other side of the ghost so she and Craig might seem to be talking to one another.

"I can help you end this," he explained. "I can help you move on."

An automated announcement boomed out, and a waft of warm air ruffled Craig's hair, heralding the arrival of the next train. Craig spoke more urgently to get through to the girl. Tara kept talking to him cheerfully until he gestured for her to stop. It was too distracting. He didn't care if people thought he was a nutcase.

"Please," he said. "What do you have to lose?"

The ghost shook her head.

"I have no choice. I did this to my family. My mother. My sister. I don't deserve any rest. No heaven for me."

This was nothing new to Craig.

"If they knew that you're still here, what would they say? That you should go on suffering? Think about the love they still have for you. Remember them. What would they say?"

The dead woman put her hands over her face. The noise of the approaching train masked her sobs, but her shoulders heaved. Craig reached out, focusing on the portal he must create. The train roared into the station as the glowing vortex appeared above the ghost's head. It was slightly different this time, not just a swirl of blue-white light but throwing out golden sparks. She looked up, sensing the change, and stared open-mouthed into the portal. Craig eased her upward, using the ability he'd gained in the woods near Grendon Mill.

The ghost rose like a leaf dancing in the wind and was gone. The portal closed instantly, leaving Craig with the lingering impression of black lettering on pink.

"Happy Times," he murmured.

"Is it gone?" Tara asked.

The train came to a halt, and they stepped back as its doors slid open.

"Yeah, she's gone," he said.

They joined the flow of passengers heading for the escalator.

CHAPTER 15

GRAY MARKET

"Maybe your power is evolving. Developing in some way," Tara suggested.

They were making their way through the streets of Camden. It was a busy, Bohemian area with lots of quirky shops and open-air markets. The sun was out, but the mid-morning temperature was balmy. The atmosphere was good-humored, with food stalls and buskers livening up the scene. Craig glimpsed a pair of his first British bobbies walking slowly in the distance, apparently sharing banter with street vendors. He had seen no more ghosts, so far as he could tell. But given the crowded sidewalks, they'd be easy to miss.

"I don't know," Craig said. "I've moved on a couple of dozen souls since I got the power. The portal always seemed the same. But things changed with Leroy. I think I saw his mother. And now, those sparks. They were pretty and all, but they were new. What if the power is failing, not developing?"

"Or it's growing stronger," she countered with a smile. "You have to start thinking the glass is half full, Craig."

She took his hand, and they walked like that for a few dozen yards before she let go to shoot some video. He felt suddenly resentful of their fake vlogger personas. If they were up against the Shadow Trust, why bother with deception? An outfit that had been around for more than a century wasn't going to fall for a basic ruse on social media. Still, it justified snooping around and asking a lot of questions.

They'd moved into a large square taken up almost entirely by market stalls. The square was surrounded by rows of small shops selling clothes, books, used furniture, and in a few cases, food. There was also a pub at one corner. This was the rendezvous location, and they threaded their way toward it through the ambling crowds. As they got closer, Craig saw the name in gold letters.

The Slaughtered Lamb.

A traditional inn sign also hung above the entrance. It did not depict slaughter of any kind. Instead, it bore a picture of a pot on an old-fashioned hearth, with steam escaping from under the lid. A small mercy, but he was grateful. The doors of the pub were closed. As Craig stepped up to them, he saw the interior was dark.

"They're not open yet," Tara explained, "but we can get upstairs."

She led him around to a side door. Peeling blue paint revealed a layer of sickly green underneath. It looked like the ideal entrance to a place to do some murky business. Tara pressed a buzzer, waited about five seconds, and then pressed it again. A voice crackled from the speaker.

"All right, all right, don't wear the bloody thing out!"

The buzzer sounded again, and there was a click. Tara led him inside, and the door swung shut behind them. The stairway was unlit. Tara flicked on the flashlight on her phone, and they made their way upstairs. The walls were half-covered in floral wallpaper that was peeling away from ancient brickwork. Underfoot, a threadbare carpet couldn't prevent the echo of their footsteps. It was the ideal place for an ambush. Tara had the same thought, as the iron brooch detached itself from her denim jacket and spun through the air above them.

"Ooh, very fancy," said a voice ahead. "I like a bit of the old

82

psychokinesis."

"You Abdul?" Tara asked.

"That's my name, don't wear it out!" came the reply in a bad imitation of an American accent.

Craig rounded the corner onto a narrow landing to see a stocky man with immensely broad shoulders. This Brit clearly worked out and had added a lot of muscle to a naturally powerful frame. Abdul's face was partially concealed by a massive beard that made his hairless scalp look all the balder. He was wearing faded gym gear that looked like it might rip at the seams at any moment. He smiled through his facial hair, and Craig relaxed a little.

"You must be Craig, right? See any ghosts around here?"

Craig glanced around the confined space.

"No."

"Good. I've got some defenses up, but you can never totally rely on them," Abdul explained, turning to head through an open doorway. "These ghosts, always spying on people turning an honest living."

Abdul lived in the flat above the pub. It was a cozy, if shabby, apartment, half-filled with boxes bearing various brand names. Some, like Coors and Budweiser, were familiar to Craig. Others were either British or from elsewhere in Europe. There was also an array of weights in one corner. The air smelled of stale sweat and a hint of beer. Abdul, he thought, might not be a very strict Muslim.

"Sorry about the mess, but this is my stock in trade, and storage is a bit tricky at the mo," Abdul said, seeing Craig looking around. "My proper job is supplying booze and crisps and stuff to a few pubs around here. I get it cheap, but it goes on the landlord's books at the regular price, so that's a nice little earner for all concerned."

He grinned again and gestured to a sagging sofa. They sat side by side, and Craig wondered if they were supposed to pose as a couple to this Brit. He dismissed the thought as Tara asked matter-of-factly if Abdul had the gear.

"Of course. I never fail to complete an order."

He lifted a box of Czech lager as if it weighed nothing and dropped it onto an armchair. Underneath was a metal strongbox decorated with a camo pattern. Abdul picked it up with the same insouciance, set it in front of them, and unfastened a combination lock.

"Feel free to inspect the goods; Mr. Stark paid through the nose for a lot of this stuff."

Craig leaned forward. Inside was an impressive array of weapons. He picked up a BB pistol. Underneath was a box of iron pellets. Tara was trying the edge of an iron dagger against her thumb. Seeing this, Abdul chuckled.

"Does it matter how sharp it is if you're going to chuck it at a ghost?"

"It matters if I want to stab a demon," she replied, unsmiling. "What do you think, Craig?"

Craig was impressed. As well as four daggers and two guns with ammo, there were a couple of tasers and various lesser supplies. Iron filings in plastic containers, salt and herbs in jars, and some less-identifiable items. And there was a new addition to the arsenal. Wielding daggers in public had its drawbacks, so Craig had suggested something less conspicuous but still effective on ghosts. Stark's supplier had obliged with a very British solution: two compact umbrellas with thick iron handles.

"This is more than we had in Grendon Mill," he said. "I'm impressed."

He almost added that it was a pity there weren't three sets of weapons so Shane could be fully equipped but bit his tongue. Abdul would undoubtedly report back to Stark. Any hint of a third party involved in their mission might endanger them all. Instead, he picked up an umbrella and fumbled for the catch. It shot out to three feet in length. Holding it by the wrong end with the struts still furled, it made a club with a good reach.

"Yeah, this will do fine," Tara agreed. "What about transport?"

Abdul, who'd been squatting by the steel box, stood up.

"It's in a lockup around the corner. You still got your UK driving license?"

"Of course," Tara replied. "Let's get moving."

They replaced the weapons except for the umbrellas. After locking the box, Abdul easily hefted it onto one beefy shoulder. They followed him downstairs and back out into Camden Market. The first thing Craig saw was a ghost who was dressed in early twentieth-century clothes, with a narrow-brimmed hat, and carrying an old-fashioned furled umbrella. He raised the umbrella and pointed it at Craig, who raised his own umbrella to point.

"Ghost," he said quietly. "About ten yards."

A few passersby looked curiously at the little group. One girl laughed, probably at the sight of him wielding an umbrella. The sky was a spotless azure dome. The spirit approached, passing through the laughing girl, whose expression changed to one of surprise.

"That was weird," she said to her friend, and the two walked on.

The ghost hesitated and then stopped. An elderly woman talking on her phone walked through him. The woman stopped speaking and stumbled, clutching her chest. The ghost remained immobile. Abdul put down his burden and rushed forward, asking the woman if she was okay.

"I think I just had a funny turn, love," the lady replied as the big man put an arm around her. "I'll be all right if I can just have a little sit-down."

Craig walked toward the ghost, holding his umbrella with the handle pointing forward. The ghost retreated a few paces and held up a hand.

"I'm just here to deliver a message, old boy," said the spirit. "Don't shoot the messenger."

The ghost's accent was almost comically posh like a character from an old British movie. Rather than reply, Craig stood still and waited. Tara moved beside him and took his arm.

"Hey honey, is that creepy guy still around?" she asked.

"Yeah, I can see him," Craig replied. "He says he has a message. Probably the same thing as last night."

"You people need to wake up and smell that coffee you keep going on about, you know," the ghost said. "That girly you're with is a liability, but that's not the worst of it. You're helping to create a truly ghastly situation."

Craig relayed the essentials of the little speech to Tara, then spoke to the ghost.

"You need to piss off…"

A passerby walked between them and the ghost, giving Craig a quizzical look. It was too crowded for an exchange of insults, let alone a conversation. Abdul had returned after escorting the woman to a coffee shop.

"That bastard still hanging around?" he asked. "It's awkward, but maybe if we went out of sight of the market…"

He picked up the weapons box and led them into an alley. At the end of it was a garage door secured by an old-fashioned padlock. The ghost, as Craig had anticipated, followed them, still warning of terrible consequences if they didn't quit.

"Could you be any less specific, buddy?" Craig said sarcastically. "You sound like a bad fortune cookie."

As Abdul opened the garage door, Craig and Tara turned to

confront the spirit. The ghost kept well back as they extended the handles of their umbrellas. Craig felt vaguely ridiculous, thinking of Mary Poppins and Harry Potter.

"Okay, say your piece and get lost," Tara demanded, sending her brooch drifting toward the interloper.

The ghost moved back a few more feet.

"I only know that some significant beings are very worried about you Americans messing around on our patch," he said. "They don't want to reveal themselves, being discreet coves. Also, they think it devalues the currency to always manifest on the earthly plane, don't you know? Point is, they want you to leave old Blighty and let someone better qualified handle the problem."

Craig did his best to sum up this diatribe.

"Bollocks!" shouted Abdul, although he couldn't see the spirit. "You're just a mercenary little twat who's been offered a benefit for harassing these nice people. Bugger off!"

The ghost shook his head in what might have been genuine sadness.

"If I told you that you were helping to assemble one of those dreadful atomic bombs, you'd stop and think," he said, "but what you are doing could be even worse. The higher powers tell me you are serving what seems to be a man, but who is in fact the shadow cast by the abomination."

CHAPTER 16

GHOSTS OF OLD LONDON TOWN

Craig passed on this message word for word. Tara looked unimpressed, and Abdul remained stony-faced.

"Is that all?" Craig demanded. "Because we've got a job to do. Do you want me to help you move on? I have that power."

"Good Lord, no!"

The ghost looked horrified at the suggestion. Craig snapped out the handle of the umbrella and strode forward quickly. The ghost retreated but not quite fast enough, and a sweeping blow made it vanish, leaving behind a faint cry that might have been, "Oh dear!"

"Gone," Craig said. "Caught him off-guard."

"Silly bugger," Abdul grunted. "Anyway, what do you think of your wheels?"

The wheels in question belonged to a red Ford Kuga.

"Thought you'd like something to remind you of home. Sorry I couldn't make it left-hand drive," the big man said.

"That's okay," Tara said, walking to the driver's side.

While she was familiarizing herself with the SUV, Craig asked Abdul about the ghost's warning. The phrase "shadow cast by the abomination" had seemed to mean something to the bodybuilder, but Abdul was cagey and just shrugged his oversized shoulders.

"Look, mate, all that stuff is way above my pay grade. I do a job, I get paid. Maybe the world ends; maybe somebody gets a bit annoyed. I know, it's not exactly moral, and I feel I'm letting my old mum down when I overlook something dodgy. But how else can you earn a living these days? Be ethical, and you end up living in a ditch, eating grass."

While Craig didn't entirely agree with the Londoner's outlook, he was hardly in a position to criticize. He persisted, though, to get some information.

"Did the ghost mean that Stark isn't human?"

Abdul made a "Who knows?" gesture.

"He's a good customer, that's all I know for sure. I've never met him, and as far as I know, he's never been to Europe. You hear rumors, though. He's supposed to have this special place. Like a chamber, underground, you know? He keeps all sorts of weird stuff in it."

Craig made an encouraging noise. Abdul looked around nervously.

"Nobody to overhear," Craig said, scrutinizing their surroundings.

Abdul lowered his voice, and Craig leaned closer to listen.

"Way I heard it, he doesn't just collect objects. He has something else in there. Something alive, in a way."

Tara started the Kuga and edged it forward out of the garage. As if this were a cue to return to normal, Abdul stepped back from Craig and grinned at her, giving a thumbs-up sign. Then, he put the box in the back. Tara asked for a dagger and a taser, which Abdul provided. She put them in the glovebox.

"Thanks for everything," Craig called as the man stood back.

Craig was about to slam the passenger door when saw the ghost in the rear-view mirror. It was a man, probably, but it was hard to tell. This one had died in a fire, and its blackened body was still trailing wisps of greasy smoke. It was shambling out of the garage, right behind Abdul. Craig shouted a warning and then grabbed the dagger from the glovebox.

In that short time, another ghost appeared. This one was bearing down on them from ahead and to the right. It, too, showed signs of a violent death, with its head lolling to one side. Its clothes were archaic, and Craig guessed it had been hanged sometime long ago.

Craig gestured with the dagger at the first ghost and yelled at Abdul to move toward him. The Londoner was not fast enough. The spirit flung itself forward and almost vanished inside the bodybuilder's huge torso. Abdul made a choking sound, and his face took on an expression of surprise. It would have been comical if he hadn't been dying. Craig covered the few yards in seconds but couldn't use the dagger. Instead, he had to circle Abdul looking for a target. He saw a lank, crisped leg and jabbed at it. The ghost disappeared to wherever its haunted item was. Abdul recovered, throwing himself forward onto the concrete. The ghost reappeared and lunged at Craig, its fire-blackened fingers clutching at his chest. He felt the pressure of fingers inside his body, seeking to crush his heart. The pain was bad but bearable.

He'd had worse. Many times.

"Sorry, buddy," he gasped, as he brought the dagger around behind the ghost's skull. "You can't win this one."

The burned man disappeared as the blade pierced its brain. Craig took a second to recover. Tara had extended the handle of her umbrella and was flailing it energetically while her brooch circled her like a tiny drone. The other ghost darted back and forth but didn't risk coming too close. Craig shouted directions as he circled the car, and Tara hurled the umbrella but missed. The ghost retreated through the wall of the pub.

"Help Abdul while I keep watch," Craig said.

Tara knelt beside their contact, who was lying face-down.

"I think he's breathing, but I can't turn him over," she cried.

Craig shoved the dagger into his waistband, grazing himself in his haste, and went to help. Abdul weighed a ton, but they finally rolled him onto his back. He wouldn't come around, however, and they decided that they couldn't leave him. Tara called 999, the British emergency number, and heard that an ambulance might take up to an hour.

"The NHS has gone downhill," she ranted, ending the call. "We'll have to take him to the ER."

"Moving him could be bad," Craig pointed out.

"No choice!" she shot back, running past the Kuga into the square and shouting. "Hey, bit of help here, please?"

Tara found a young couple who was willing to help lift Abdul. Craig concocted a story about their friend having a heart condition. The trip to the nearest ER was nerve-wracking, but once they arrived, the staff swung efficiently into action. Abdul had a phone and a driver's license on him. Tara told the doctor on duty that they didn't really know the guy, which was true enough. The friendly Londoner had just been helping out a couple of tourists.

"We can't hang around indefinitely," Tara said after Abdul had been whisked away on a gurney. "And it's not like we can do anything meaningful to help."

"What if they track him down?" Craig asked and then realized it was a foolish question.

They couldn't protect Abdul. London, maybe the whole island, had to be considered hostile territory. The sooner they got the job over with, the quicker they could get home. They left contact details at the hospital reception and left.

They were halfway back to their hotel before Craig remembered the first ghost's warning. Chloe had spoken about missiles hidden under Siberian snow. Was it a coincidence that the messenger had used the analogy of assembling a nuclear bomb?

"Probably," he muttered.

"What?" Tara asked.

"Oh, it might be nothing, but…"

He told her, and she looked thoughtful, then cursed as a delivery rider darted out from a side street.

"Goddamn… yeah, it probably is a coincidence. Happens all the time."

They had plenty to preoccupy them, and lingering thoughts of Armageddon soon gave way to mundane concerns like packing and lunch. They checked out of the hotel around midday and found a pub on the outskirts of London that served fish and chips. Craig enjoyed the meal, which was served by a cheerful and talkative barmaid. Their accents naturally triggered a spate of questions, and even the most mundane answers seemed to delight their server. When they mentioned ghost hunting, the woman became almost ecstatic.

"Ooh," she said. "We've got a ghost! This pub's famous for being haunted. Sometimes, when you come in in the morning, there's things been moved around. You know, glasses and bottles and even furniture. They say he's a former landlord who was in cahoots with the highwaymen around these parts. Oh, and I think he pinched my bum once."

The conversation meandered on, with Tara doing most of the heavy lifting. Craig, meanwhile, had identified three ghosts in the bar. One could have been the aforementioned landlord. The man was plump and red-faced and wore a slightly lopsided wig with curls and a ribbon. He was standing behind a couple of young guys who were playing a slot machine. Perhaps the old guy had been a gambler in life.

The other ghosts were very different. One was an insubstantial presence, only a vague outline that seemed to drift between the doorway and a window seat. By contrast, the last ghost that Craig spotted might have been mistaken for a living person. It was an elderly woman in modern clothes who stood behind the bar. At first, he had mistaken her for a staff member, but then the cheerful barmaid had walked straight at her, and the woman had vanished, only to reappear in the same spot a moment later.

Craig had long since perfected the art of studying ghosts while appearing not to see them. When he went to use the bathroom, he looked up from the sink to see the old lady standing behind him.

"Why won't you be told?" she asked. "We don't want you here."

CHAPTER 17

THE OTHER PLACE

"You don't want me in the pub?" Craig asked. "Because we'll be on our way right now, I think."

"You know what I mean," the ghost said.

The woman seemed peevish rather than angry. Her tone might have been used on a child who'd just hit a ball into her garden, but Craig was cautious. He had the dagger in his waistband, behind his back, and concealed by his jacket. He turned to face the ghost and reached slowly around to grasp the hilt of the weapon. But first, he decided to take a shot in the dark.

"I know about the Shadow Trust."

The ghost stared and then laughed.

"You think you know," she jeered, "but they didn't send me. I'm telling you for your own good, you young idiot."

Craig pulled out the dagger. The ghost looked at it and then back at Craig.

"Things have come to a fine state of affairs when a strapping young man threatens a helpless old lady."

"Yeah, but this is the men's washroom, not an ATM," Craig pointed out. "Plus, you're already dead. And I've had enough of ominous warnings. Get lost. Or do you want me to move you on?"

For the first time, the ghost looked surprised, then meditative.

"Ah, so it is true. There's been talk of a seer who's invulnerable to us. That was hard to credit, so I didn't believe you had the power."

"You'd better believe it..."

Loud voices sounded in the short corridor just outside. Craig had replaced the knife in his waistband by the time the door banged open, and two middle-aged men walked in. The ghost stepped back as one walked straight at her, oblivious. Craig nodded politely and washed his hands a second time, wondering if the ghost would hang around.

At first, he thought she had given up as she faded into a wall. But then, as he made his way back to their table, he heard her whispering urgently.

"If you can move me on to a better place, I'll tell you something you should know. About *him*."

Craig could guess who she meant. Tara, sensing something was up, quietly asked him what was going on. He explained the situation and suggested they try outside. The Kuga was at the far end of the parking lot. The SUV was big enough to screen them from anyone using the pub's entrance, and there was a high fence on the other side. The ghost had tagged along, fading slightly in the sunlight but still visible to Craig.

"Okay," he said when they were out of sight. "What do you want to tell me?"

"Promise me first," the dead woman said. "Swear you'll send me to another place. The good place."

"As for 'good', I can't guarantee, but I'll help you move on," Craig said. "But first, give me the info."

The dead woman seemed undecided, and Craig could imagine her mulling over the options. She had presumably failed to move on herself and had never met anyone able to help. And might never again.

"She still here?" Tara asked.

"Yeah," he said. "She's the cranky type. Takes a jaundiced view of things, so doesn't want to help us even a little. I guess we'd better get going."

"All right, all right!" the ghost protested. "You'd better keep your side of the bargain."

Craig folded his arms and waited.

"Stark," the woman said. "Stark is not a man at all, but a man-shaped shadow of something terrible and ancient. Something incomplete. It was torn apart, dismembered ages ago. And it's been searching ever since to put itself together again."

"Like Frankenstein?" Craig scoffed. "Sounds unlikely."

The ghost jabbed a bony finger at his chest.

"Fool! You don't know the half of it. Once this thing heals itself, it will run wild. It thrives on suffering. It hates the whole world because it was maimed and left powerless for so long. And you're helping it grow strong again. Stop, if you've got any sense."

Craig relayed this to Tara, who looked skeptical but also worried.

"Gossip," she said. "Ghost gossip, admittedly, but still just tittle-tattle."

The ghost stared at her with contempt and then dismissed her and came closer to Craig.

"I told you what I know," she pleaded. "Now keep your side of the bargain."

Craig sighed and tried to relax. Traffic roared nearby, and he heard someone laughing raucously as they left the pub. A car door slammed, and an engine started. But once he'd focused on the task, all the extraneous noises receded, and he was left with the sunlight and the spirit standing before him. He reached out.

The vortex that opened was barely visible against the nearly clear sky with its scatter of fluffy clouds. The blueness of the paranormal merged with that of nature. But, as before, a few golden sparks sprayed from the edge of the portal. Craig tried not to get distracted, emptying his mind of all unnecessary thoughts and controlling his emotions. He needed to concentrate, but not too much. That was the key.

The ghost of the woman started to drift upward. As she did so, the whirlpool of light became easier to make out against the sky. It darkened to a pinkish hue and then became a fiery red. Now, it was throwing out fiery orange sparks. The ghost, who had been looking at Craig, switched her gaze upward and emitted a shriek.

"No! No, don't! I don't want to remember."

Craig's concentration faltered, but the portal continued to grow. It was now about two feet across, and it was emitting sounds. Cries, moans, and howls that suggested pain but also hinted at a kind of maniacal joy. A dark hole formed in the circle of crimson light and grew until he could see what was on the other side. It was a small bedroom that looked out onto a suburban street. A couple of small, old-fashioned cars passed outside. It was England, presumably, a few decades ago.

Then Craig's attention switched to the man in the bed. He looked about sixty but might have been younger, and he seemed ill. The man was gray-faced, with several days' growth of beard and bloodshot eyes. He wore striped pajamas and a shabby dressing gown. Craig realized he was seeing things from the old woman's viewpoint as he laid a tray in front of the man. It bore just one item: a bowl of gray, watery-looking oatmeal.

"Now eat your porridge, dear. You must keep up your strength."

The man mumbled something.

"We don't want to go bothering Doctor Fordyce just because you're a little under the weather, now, do we?"

As the woman left the room, Craig detected her thoughts. She was worried that it was taking too long, and the dosage was not high enough. But she was also aware that too much weedkiller could be detected if there was an autopsy. She felt angry with the man for not simply dying and leaving her the money and the house. Above all, Craig sensed how little she felt for her victim and the terrible wrongness of the crime. She was self-absorbed and devoid of compassion.

"No! They said you moved them on to a good place!"

He was back in the parking lot. Instead of rising, the vortex had begun descending toward her. The dark hole in the center was now occupied by something hard to make out. At first, Craig thought it was a single, weird organism. Then, he realized that it was a great mass of bodies, mutilated and distorted, clutching and writhing, biting and punching and kicking. A moment later, he grasped the truth. The people on the other side of the portal were one organism in a sense. They merged into each other like conjoined twins but far worse.

The merging had been messy, perhaps deliberately so. Bodily fluids leaked and blood mingled with excrement. A length of yellow intestine dangled and was gnawed upon. Exposed brain tissue was scooped out and swallowed. Mad with pain and ravenous with hunger, the foul network of what had been humans tortured themselves.

It was obscene and impossible in his world, but it seemed more real to Craig than everyday reality. And far more horrific.

"Stop!" the ghost pleaded. "No, I don't want to go there! I don't deserve it. I deserve a second chance!"

Craig tried to end the process, but it made no difference. This was something new, a portal that, once opened, became independent of his will. It shimmered and flung out small bolts of energy as it sank and covered the ghost's fear-contorted features. As the ring of flame descended, the dead woman disappeared.

The portal collapsed into a tiny glowing ember and was gone.

"Bad trip?" Tara asked as Craig leaned against the car door, gasping.

He didn't want to look her in the eye, but it beat seeing his reflection in the tinted glass.

"I think I just sent someone to Hell, so, yeah."

CHAPTER 18

NORTH BY NORTHWEST

They had to get going. They agreed on that. If they stuck to the mission and got it over with, they could go home. After that brief conversation, Craig sat in silence for half an hour while Tara got them onto a road called the A1. It sounded classy, but it proved to be a dull highway beset by traffic jams. When congestion cleared and they could push the speed limit, which was seventy, Craig noticed something strange.

"Why is this road so curvy?" he asked.

Tara thought about it for a moment.

"Oh, yeah, I remember now. When the Brits were building these motorways, they looked at the German autobahns and our freeways and thought, 'No thanks.' They were worried about highway hypnosis, you know? So they built in gentle curves so you have to keep alert and steer just a little. It's clever psychology, I guess."

Craig tried to focus on the mundane world where road safety was a serious, sensible issue, but he kept remembering the portal. Or more precisely, what lay beyond it. He had never glimpsed anything that might be called Heaven. Now, he had seen Hell, or perhaps one of many hells. From now on, he might inflict eternal torment on a human soul. They no doubt deserved it, but that was not the point. He wanted to help people, not act as a cosmic judge handing out sentences.

Craig told Tara how he felt, stumbling over some concepts and not finding the right words. She listened patiently, making small noises that said, "Yeah, I'm listening." When he ground to a halt, she took time to mull over the problem.

"If there is a judge, it's definitely not you," she said finally. "Those souls are predestined for good or bad places. From what I've learned—and I'm still a novice—there are many possible afterlives. What you saw seems to have been a place designed to remind those who acted selfishly of what they rejected. You know? All those bodies intertwined and in agony because of it."

Now, it was Craig's turn to ponder. Surely a more apt punishment for the nameless old woman would have been a hell of eternal loneliness? But she might have thrived in isolation. Forcing her to confront the truth about humans and their interdependence made more sense. She had committed a heinous act of selfishness, destroying a man who might well have loved her. And, as far as Craig could tell, she had not felt a qualm of conscience. Despite all that, he could not square it with what he had done, however unwittingly.

"Eternal suffering," he said. "Does anyone deserve that? I mean, apart from Hitler, maybe, guys like that?"

"How do you know it's eternal?" Tara asked.

Craig looked ahead at the curving ribbon of asphalt. The road straightened out for a minute or so. He saw the vanishing point, or rather didn't see it. He merely experienced an illusion of gazing into infinite distance. Then the motorway curved gently to the left and the illusion was gone. He hoped Tara was right. That for most souls, eternal damnation was not on the cards. But would he ever know for sure? Could any living mortal know such a thing?

"You're still going to help ghosts move on, right?" Tara asked. "Because, apart from anything else, that might be a useful bargaining chip."

"I guess," he said.

They made steady progress northward. They passed places Craig might have liked to visit under different circumstances. Nottingham inevitably made him think of Robin Hood. The road sign for Manchester seemed odd because it lacked the suffix United. He saw few ghosts, just an occasional glimpse of someone in anachronistic clothing as they sped by. But then the signs told him they were approaching York, and things changed. Ghosts became more common, some appearing in the middle of the road. None seemed hostile.

"We're on an ancient Roman road, or pretty close, anyways," Tara said. "Travelers have lived and died on this route for nearly two thousand years. Guess you're going to see a few interesting characters. Just gonna have to charge right through."

Craig imagined how many ghosts might accumulate over twenty centuries. Too many. At the same time, he was excited by the thought of seeing old-time people. He looked up York on his phone and found that it had been built by Romans, occupied by Anglo-Saxons, and conquered by Vikings. He kept a lookout, hoping for Romans, but saw no legionaries marching along the motorway. However, when he did some more Googling he found that someone else had. Or very nearly.

"Did you know this?" he asked, scrolling through a site called Britain's Greatest Ghosts. "A plumber was installing central heating down in the cellar of an old house, and he saw Roman soldiers marching past. Only, he saw them from the waist up. Oh, and he described them as looking scruffy, with stubble and dirty clothes. Like a real army on the march. That was in... 1953."

"I know the story," Tara said. "The ghost walks in the city always include it."

She sounded a little tense, her eyes fixed straight ahead. Craig remembered that she had had a bad experience in northern England,

and they were going to pass close to the place where it had happened.

"I wish I could drive and take some of the pressure off."

"Me too."

She spoke tersely.

"Sorry," she said a moment later. "You've been great. I couldn't have gotten this far without you."

"You saved my ass a few times," he reminded her.

Neither of them spoke for a while. Then Craig wondered how Shane was doing and asked.

"Why not ask him?" Tara said, this time flashing a smile.

Craig composed a text, keeping the language neutral, focusing on their status. "Nearly at destination, how are you doing?" seemed reasonable. He spent about five miles waiting for a reply before he resumed scrolling sites that dealt with the paranormal. They had done a fair amount of research on Castle McIvor, but it didn't hurt to refresh his memory.

Craig was rereading a page on a fairly sober history site. The account it gave of the laird committing the massacre was familiar. It referred in passing to claims that the supernatural had been involved, sniffily rejecting them as mere gossip. The site had a link to various pieces of folklore and poetry. Craig idly clicked on one link to be confronted by a verse he found baffling.

> But I have dream'd a dreary dream,
> Beyond the Isle of Skye;
> I saw a dead man win a fight,
> And I think that man was I.

There was no obvious connection to the massacre. Craig checked and found the verse was from a longer poem about a battle between English and Scottish warlords. It had taken place a century before the killings at Castle McIvor, but someone had seen fit to link to it. He found nothing else. The words haunted him, even though the context was clear enough. The Scottish warlord, the Earl of Douglas, had been mortally wounded, but his men had still defeated the English. The idea of a dead man winning a fight was too powerful given what Craig had seen and done. He closed the browser, leaned back, and closed his eyes.

"Well, that was York," Tara observed. "Blink and you'll miss it. It's such a small city that all that history kind of spills out over the edges."

"Yeah, I guess."

Craig opened his eyes and blinked. The sun was low on the western horizon. They had lost time in traffic jams and would not make it to Newcastle before nightfall. Another historic city, of course. The "new" castle it was named after was nine hundred years old and change. Craig would have preferred to skirt the place, but Tara needed to rest. More ghosts seemed inevitable. With luck, they would be friendly.

"I'll have to keep watch," he said. "Maybe grab some coffee? For me, I mean."

"Okey-dokey."

Ten minutes later, they were in the parking lot of a small mall that contained a Burger King, a Subway, the inevitable Starbucks, and some British stores whose names he didn't recognize. Tara had a Diet Coke while Craig went for strong, black coffee. There were no ghosts around at first. This was apparently a new road, built where only a few farm tracks had existed. Craig checked his phone again, but all he found were new junk emails.

"Hello!"

The little girl was holding a teddy bear. The stuffed toy showed signs of having been dragged along, probably over a muddy field. The girl might have been four or five. She had bangs, pigtails with red ribbons, and a dark blue dress. No shoes. She looked up at him without any sign of hostility, but she didn't seem friendly, either. Her brown eyes were huge in the way only a child's can be, at least in real life. There were traces of what looked like dried mud on one side of her face. He pictured her being pushed down and forced into the dirt by someone.

"We got a visitor?" Tara said quietly, looking past the girl.

It was good to have that confirmation, though he hardly needed it.

"Yeah. A small one."

He gave the child a wave.

"Hello!"

The girl lifted her teddy bear, pressing the dirty muzzle to one pink ear. Then she looked up at Craig again.

"Jeffrey says your friend got his car back. And a lot of bad people are very upset."

"I can help…" Craig began, but the girl had already vanished.

CHAPTER 19

SEARCHING FOR ANSWERS

"But why couldn't I help her? She was a victim; I'm sure of it. She deserved to go to a better place."

Craig was talking to himself, not seeing the road signs or the traffic.

"It wasn't her time, I guess, or she didn't want to move on," Tara said. "She delivered a message to you. To us."

Craig peered out of the passenger side window as they overtook a tour bus full of elderly passengers. A few were asleep, their heads lolling. Others held animated conversations. One or two stared at their phones.

"Don't feel bad because somebody else suffered in life," Tara went on. "Seriously. I've seen some bad things, and I've played the blame game with myself. I'm still playing it. I know it's pointless. We can only do our best."

"And hope for the best," he added. "Yeah. I guess."

Tara flashed him a smile before fixing her attention back on the road.

"Hey, here's a thing. Finding a common factor. Why do some people die in the Red Chamber while others don't? We've got at least another hour before we get there. Why not look at the facts again?"

Craig felt slightly sheepish. He had not taken a very close look at the legend the first time; he had been preoccupied with packing and worrying. Tara, though, methodical as always, had prepared a file on the deaths in the Red Chamber. He took out his phone and opened it. The file consisted of a summary in pdf format that listed the basic facts. There were also shots of web pages and a few other documents she had downloaded.

Tara had found records of eleven mysterious deaths in the Red Chamber. All had occurred on July 12, but at different times of the day or night. The most recent death was during World War II, which explained why the room could be booked now. Many people assumed the curse, if it ever existed, had spent its power. Or the ghost of Angus McIvor had gotten bored and moved on. Both were possible, Craig thought. Hope for the best, sure. But prepare for the worst.

He started checking the background on the deaths, beginning with the most recent. He found to his surprise that the victim had been American. Commander Frank Belknap had been serving with the U.S. Navy in Britain, and he had taken a week's leave in July 1944. Unwisely, he had accepted a bet from a fellow officer to sleep in the Red Chamber on that fateful night. The stake had been fifty dollars, an impressive sum at the time. When the friend—who was sleeping in another room—checked, Belknap's body was cold. The coroner's verdict was heart failure. No autopsy was carried out, and the body had been shipped back home for burial.

"Interesting," Craig murmured.

"Is that the Navy guy?" Tara asked.

"Yeah. Took a gamble and lost. Nobody has died since then, though?"

"Nope," Tara said. "But remember, for decades, nobody could sleep in that room on the 12th. They only revoked that rule eight years ago. So far, nobody has died."

Craig went back to the earliest death. This was the year after the massacre, when a distant cousin of Laird Angus had inherited his lands, titles, and, of course, the castle. The new laird had brought a young bride and insisted on sleeping in the main bedchamber. On the anniversary of the killings, Lady McIvor had been awakened by her husband clutching her shoulder and trying to speak. He had died a moment later, his face contorted with pain and terror. Naturally, the lady was asked what she had seen, but she never spoke again. Not a single word.

"Struck dumb, wow," Craig said. "This is hardcore folklore. But how reliable is an account from the sixteenth century? Hell, Columbus was making news while this was going on."

"Those accounts are pretty reliable," Tara replied. "Keep reading."

The Red Chamber had been left vacant for more than a century, but during violent upheavals in the mid-seventeenth century, the curse had worked its evil again. The first death had been recorded in a few lines, but this time, there was a more detailed account. It was puzzling because it concerned religious politics, which seemed to have been pretty hardcore at the time.

"Who were the Covenanters?" he asked.

"Militant Presbyterians," Tara replied. "Fiercely anti-Catholic, keen on witch burning, and generally humorless. Good soldiers, though. They rose against the king of England, and that helped trigger a wider rebellion supported by the English parliament. There were a series of civil wars. Total mayhem."

"I get that," Craig said. "So this guy, Colonel Brodie, was a Covenanter, and his regiment occupied the castle because the laird at the time supported the king. But why would Brodie sleep in the Red Chamber?"

"Read on," Tara suggested.

Craig skimmed some of the political stuff and found the

relevant passage.

> *It was on the 10th of July in the ill-fated year of 1642 that Colonel Brodie and his dragoons took possession of the castle, taking the garrison by surprise and suffering no casualties. The colonel treated the laird, his family, and servants fairly, if somewhat sternly. However, by some ill luck while breakfasting with his captives, the colonel was told the legend of the Red Chamber. His devotion to scripture and deep antipathy to Papist superstition...*

"What's 'Papist' mean?" Craig asked.

"Catholic," Tara said, and he resumed reading.

> *... antipathy to Papist superstition led Colonel Brodie to declare that curses, hauntings, and such were against the word of God, who commands all things. Despite the best efforts of the laird to dissuade him, the colonel swore that he would sleep in the fateful bedchamber and did so. The McIvors and even his officers sought to change Brodie's mind many times in the subsequent days, but the colonel was adamant. And on the night of the 12th, he retired to the Red Chamber, declaring loudly that he would not be cowed by any specter but would have at it with his sword and see what such beings were made of.*

Craig had to chuckle at that. The guy had balls. But the next paragraph was sobering.

> *It lacked some minutes to midnight when the household was roused by a great commotion coming from the colonel's*

chamber. One of his most loyal comrades had, without Brodie's knowledge, taken up station outside the door, and he entered at once. The officer found the colonel lying on the floor, sword in hand, his eyes unblinking. The young man asked his commander what ailed him. All Brodie could say was, "Blue. A blue man." And then the colonel suffered a terrible seizure, and his soul departed his mortal frame.

"So… he blamed a member of the Blue Man Group?"

"Weird, right?" Tara laughed. "The other accounts are less interesting because none of the victims had a chance to say anything. They were all just found dead the following morning."

Craig read on as the sun sank toward a range of hills a few miles to the west. Nobody slept in the Red Chamber on July 12 for decades, though the room was used the rest of the year. But somebody inevitably had to show off. In 1758, it was Captain Wentworth of the Royal Navy, whose lifeless body was found on the morning of the 13th. In 1814, a Regency eccentric, Sir Miles Formby, accepted a wager to sleep in the room. His death led to a minor scandal, as some suspected he'd been murdered for an inheritance. But the investigation found no hint of foul play, and there was not a single mark on his body.

There were also two instances of people testing the curse and surviving. In 1794, Lady Margery Fitzroy slept in the Red Chamber on the 12th and ate a hearty breakfast the next morning. Three years later, a German traveler pulled off the same feat. It was in part because of these successes that Formby tried his luck. During all this time, however, the McIvor family shunned the room on the key date. Formby's body was the one reportedly taken by body snatchers. The one with the lethal wound to the heart, despite having no sign of a wound on his flesh.

"So why did Sir Miles die while those other two survived?" Craig asked.

Tara shrugged.

"Beats me. I was hoping you could bring a fresh insight to the data because I'm stumped."

Between Sir Miles Formby and Commander Belknap, dozens of men and women had braved the Red Chamber. It became a kind of game for eminent Victorians. A few turned down the chance. Among the latter was Charles Dickens, who declared that he "didn't believe in curses but was not fool enough to risk his life as he might be wrong." Dickens was proved right a couple of years later when the room claimed another victim, Henry Wilkinson. He was a celebrated ghost hunter who planned to talk to the specter in the Red Chamber. As one newspaper wryly commented, "It seems the ghost was not impressed by Mr. Wilkie's repartee."

"So, what did they have in common?" Craig asked. "Two naval officers and one soldier, but what about the others?"

He started Googling to find out more about the victims. Sir Miles Formby had been a gambler with a reputation for chasing anything in a skirt. He had fought two duels, both against jealous husbands. In one case, he had killed the other man and had had to leave the country for a while. Craig checked the guy's title and found that he was a Knight of the Order of St. George.

"A knight, and he killed a guy in a fight with a sword," Craig said. "So, if this Wilkinson guy was a soldier or something like it…"

"Yeah, I thought that," Tara said, "but information on him is scant. No mention of him being in the Army or Navy. Or doing anything violent."

Craig searched some more. Several sites mentioned Wilkinson's death, but often as a footnote in the wider story of the Red Chamber. The guy was basically a footnote, and Craig felt bad for him. Then, he had a stroke of luck. A link from an obscure site led him to a blog by one of Wilkinson's distant relatives. The blogger had posted a faded and badly creased photograph of the man.

It was a lousy picture that showed a middle-aged man with side whiskers and a chunky mustache wearing typical Victorian clothing. Something interesting, though. Craig enlarged the image and zoomed in on the lapel of Wilkinson's coat. There was a ribbon, no doubt colored in real life, but now three shades of gray. Probably red, white, and blue, Craig thought. The ribbon bore a symbol of crossed swords and a small crown.

Craig screenshotted the symbol and did an image search. Several possibilities were flagged, but the one that scored highest was for something called the Royal Essex Regiment of Militia. Henry Wilkinson had served his country, then. Maybe that had killed him.

He turned to Tara.

"We'll need to tell Shane he'll be the number one target if he gets here in time for the big night."

CHAPTER 20

INTO THE BORDERLANDS

"Okay," Tara said after Craig had explained, "I think I count as a warrior. I've taken some lives, one way or another. Quite a few. You should know the details."

Tara told him more about the haunted house not far from Newcastle. She and Marcus Mortlake had gone there to investigate what they thought was a malicious poltergeist, but things had gotten far worse when an ancient, nameless being had possessed Tara and triggered her latest telekinetic abilities.

"One of the workers, Carl, died. Burned up. I hardly knew him. He was just a regular working-class British guy doing a job. And the thing that took control of me killed him."

The Carl in her dream during our flight… Craig remembered.

Tara spoke without emotion, but Craig was sure her matter-of-fact tone concealed a lot.

"You were possessed," he said. "Unwittingly. You didn't know what was happening."

"Yeah, that's what Marcus said."

They stared ahead at the winding highway. The setting sun cast a red glare across the landscape. Shadows lengthened, and it grew dark. On the horizon was a faint blur that quickly resolved into a city, modern buildings mingling with the pinnacles of churches and the bulk of a castle.

"There was something else," she said finally. "A few somethings."

She told him about the second possession, the one that ended her hopes of remaining in England. More men died, and she fled the UK, away from Marcus Mortlake and the entire paranormal world. The details were shocking, and under other circumstances, Craig might not have believed such a tale. But he did not doubt Tara.

"Again, though, it wasn't your fault," he insisted. "And since then, you've put up defenses. You're stronger now. Look at Grendon Mill and the way you fought there. None of those ghosts could take possession of you."

"Yeah, but none of them tried," she said sadly. "They were too crazy to think of it. And the cultists controlling them probably weren't aware of my past. At least, not in any detail. So it doesn't prove anything."

"I still have faith in you," Craig said firmly. "So far, you've not put a foot wrong. We're a team. I've got your back, and you've got mine."

More silence. They crested a ridge, and then the road took them down into a river valley. All the lights were coming on now. They hit a complex intersection dominated by one of the roundabouts Brits seemed to love. As Tara slowed, Craig saw a man hanging from a gibbet by the roadside. The ghostly image faded swiftly as they neared. Craig was too tired to ponder what kind of haunting he'd just seen. He watched the rear-view mirror, but the hanged man didn't reappear.

"So many. I never imagined," he said.

Tara gave a short, humorless laugh.

"Spooks? Well, so long as they leave us alone."

They got snarled up in traffic on the outskirts of Newcastle. Soon, the line of cars had stopped completely. Craig noticed that many vehicles were decorated with what looked like heraldic symbols. Some were black and white; others, red and white. When he pointed this out, Tara asked him to check football scores. Sure enough, a major local match had just ended, and fans were flocking out of the stadium and heading home.

"Should've checked; sorry," she sighed. "Could've taken a different route. But here we are."

Craig sent a message to the castle to explain the situation and say they might be late. There was an immediate reply from the manager, a woman named Ellen Grant. She commiserated with them and added that she would "keep a light burning in the window" for "the weary travelers".

"She seems nice," he said, imagining a sweet old Scottish lady in a tartan shawl before realizing that was absurd. "Maybe there'll be a free tot of whisky to help us sleep."

Tara laughed again.

"I don't think they give away the good stuff. Scots have a reputation for being parsimonious. Or stingy; take your pick. Presbyterians, harsh landscape… you get the picture."

Craig revised his opinion of Ellen Grant. Now, he imagined her as a thin, hatchet-faced woman of indeterminate age in a tweed suit, looking at him disapprovingly. Then he thought more seriously about how they would interact with the staff, and other guests if there were any. The cover story of being ghost-hunting YouTubers was fine. It gave them an excuse to poke about, ask questions, and haul around large cases containing weapons. With luck, they wouldn't have to use the weapons.

It was July 9th. They had booked the Red Chamber for five days. The plan, outlined by Stark, was simple. Craig would question some local ghosts. Surely, at least one would know where the sword was concealed. They'd find the weapon and go. Their fallback plan was far riskier. On the night of the 12th, Craig would confront the ghost of the murderous laird, help him to move on, and locate and retrieve the sword in the process.

Any number of things could go wrong, of course. A few psychics, real or pretend, had stayed in the Red Chamber, but none had come up with anything convincing. As far as Craig and Tara were concerned, the enemy's mindset was an unknown quantity.

"Which is why I'd like you to back me up," he said. "Your mojo with daggers and stuff is more effective than anything I can do."

It was hard to make out Tara's expression. Then, the traffic started to move, and the lights of a car heading in the opposite direction briefly revealed her face. She looked tense, tight-lipped, and narrow-eyed. The interior of the Kuga grew dark again. Her voice seemed unnaturally loud when she spoke.

"I'll be there, partner."

Craig relaxed, glad they had worked through some issues. He was checking the time when the road ahead was suddenly swarming with ghosts. Cars, trucks, and a coach seemed to plow through a horde of men, some wearing armor, and others naked. It was a battle, Craig realized, and a chaotic one at that. In close combat, swords clashed against shields, blood sprayed from gaping wounds, and spears pieced all-too-vulnerable flesh. Riderless horses reared and plunged here and there, maddened by the noise and stench of death.

And then it was gone, vanishing behind them. Craig stammered out a brief description of what he'd seen. Tara, still caught in heavy traffic, listened but had no comment. He searched on his phone for nearby battlefields. There had been dozens of clashes between the English and Scots, plus Viking raids and numerous civil conflicts. But nothing at that location, it seemed.

A forgotten battle, then. Perhaps only a skirmish. He had, after all, seen only a hundred or so men.

"There's Hadrian's Wall," Tara said excitedly. "That Game of

Thrones guy, George Whatsit, visited it once. Gave him ideas."

Craig, forgetting the ghostly battle, gazed ahead. A sign passed too quickly for him to read the long name in Latin. But he saw a number: 122. It took him a moment to realize that it referred to the year the Roman Wall was constructed. Then they saw the wall, and Craig's expectations were dashed.

"It's so small," he said, sounding every bit like a disappointed child. Tara laughed heartily this time.

"Yeah, well, anyone can build a friggin' huge wall in a fantasy saga. Real ones are harder to build and harder to maintain. It's amazing that it's still around at all after all this time."

The wall was illuminated for some of its length and looked to be about three feet high. Another sign appeared, this one referring to a "milecastle". Glad for a distraction from the challenges ahead, Craig researched the history of Roman Britain. Soon, he was deep into the military and economic policies of Emperor Hadrian, who had ordered the wall built.

"Those Celts were pretty tough," he said, scrolling through a page on Roman campaigns in Britain.

He found a site with an illustration of a battle. The artists had let their imagination range freely, showing Romans in armor and with huge shields holding off frenzied Celtic attackers. The tribesmen were naked, their long, red hair streaming in the wind as they hurled themselves at their disciplined foes. He thought back to what he'd seen on the highway. He was almost certain he had witnessed such a clash of warriors echoing through time, its antagonists trapped in an eternal battle.

It was a sobering thought. Not for the first time, Craig wondered if he, too, would be cursed to remain as a ghost at the site of his death. Maybe even repeating the mistake that got him killed. He pushed the thought out of his mind and then reclined his seat and tried to doze, but awareness of his mortality dogged his thoughts as they approached the Scottish border.

CHAPTER 21
THE CASTLE BY NIGHT

Craig was dozing fitfully when they crossed the border. When he woke again, it was dark, and the Kuga's headlights illuminated a winding country road flanked by hedgerows. There was no sign of any buildings. The narrow strip of tarmac was the only sign of civilization.

"Are we there yet?" he asked in a mock-whiny voice.

Tara laughed and started to say something. At the same moment, something shot out from under the hedge on the right. Craig had the vague impression of something low to the ground with a long tail. Tara swore and swerved, and the SUV plowed into the left-hand hedge. Craig was suddenly very conscious of his heartbeat.

"What the hell was that?"

"A pheasant, I think," Tara replied. "Or maybe a grouse. I'm not good on game birds."

She reversed onto the road, careful not to hit the opposite hedge. They resumed the drive north, moving slower now.

"A lot of the lands around here are owned by wealthy guys who invite their rich buddies over to shoot birds," she said. "They're bred for it. The birds, I mean. They fly low and fast, which makes it more sporting. Sometimes, they escape."

Craig thought about that.

"If I owned a big tract of England—sorry, Scotland—I'd find something better to do with it than slaughter friggin' birds. Sick bastards. Why can't they find a pastime that doesn't involve killing?"

"Careful what you say about that in front of the locals," Tara cautioned. "A lot of locals are employed on the big estates. Mostly as beaters. You know? They beat the bushes to flush out the birds. Skillful beaters do it so the birds fly in front of the guns. It's seasonal work, but better than nothing. People out here have a hard time, relatively speaking. A lot of young folks leave the little villages and small towns and go to the cities."

"Same everywhere, I guess," Craig said.

"How do you feel about fishing?" Tara asked. "Because that's a big seasonal employer, too. Is that a cruel sport?"

Craig thought it over. He'd enjoyed fishing with his grandpa as a boy. It had taken him far from town, to a remote area where ghosts were few and far between, but that hadn't been the only reason it had felt good. His grandfather had sensed Craig was troubled and never asked questions; he just kept telling him he'd be okay. Suddenly, Craig saw the old man's kind face looking down at him, smiling patiently, explaining for the dozenth time how to tie a fly to a hook.

"Damn," he muttered, wiping at a stray tear.

"You okay?" Tara asked.

"Yeah. Okay, this might sound dumb, but have you ever met a genuinely good person? I don't mean somebody likable or kind, I mean someone who never thought badly of anyone, never lied, never cursed, always did the right thing?"

Tara seemed puzzled.

"No, I don't think so. But I guess you have?"

"Yeah. One. He's long gone now. He gave me a lot of advice, and I guess I was just a dumb kid and didn't understand it. One thing he said, 'There's a pattern to everything if you just look for it. Find that pattern, and things might make more sense.'"

"Sounds like a wise man," Tara said. "Guess we should be

looking for the pattern with Stark. I mean, what he wants these things for."

They talked some more about their shady employer, but as before, they reached no firm conclusions. One basic question remained unanswered: How many more special jobs did Stark have in mind for them? And how far from home would they have to journey to complete them? What was his endgame?

"Maybe your ghostly pals will find out," Tara suggested. "I mean, they keep delivering messages, one way or another."

"Yeah, they do."

Craig thought again of the woman he'd sent to hell. Then, he thought back to the first time he had been gripped by a sense of purpose. He remembered the long-dead serial killer whose trophies he had found, trinkets and toys belonging to a host of missing children. Craig had burned those trophies, one by one, and the killer's ghost had howled and screamed and vanished like smoke. The children's spirits had been freed, and Craig knew those souls had gone to a better place. He had never been more certain of anything. The killer had made his bed, and he might well have to lie in it for eternity.

I did it, Craig thought. *I did the right thing. And I can do the right thing again.*

"Here we are," Tara said wearily.

A high stone wall loomed on the left, broken by a gateway flanked by stone pillars. The wrought-iron gates were open, and Tara turned onto a gravel driveway. Their route led through a small clump of trees into open ground dotted with boulders and hummocks. Ahead lay a small pattern of lights that became windows as they grew closer. The gradient grew steeper. Castle McIvor materialized in of the darkness, a squat bulk of dark stone with a single high tower to one side.

A sign warned of a narrow bridge. The Kuga left the gravel driveway, its tires rumbling on wooden planks. Craig realized that they were crossing the moat, but he couldn't see any sign of it. Then, they passed through an impressive medieval gatehouse and entered the castle courtyard. A couple of cars were parked by a large doorway, and Tara pulled up alongside them.

Several rooms on the ground floor were lit and Craig saw someone moving around. Then a curtain was pulled shut, and the figure vanished. Another, weaker light shone from a room high in the tower. He wondered if that was the Red Chamber.

"Guess this is it," Tara said, killing the engine. "See any ghosts?"

Craig got out and stretched, inhaling the cool night air with relish. It was nearly eleven at night, and he could just make out some stars overhead. He looked around the courtyard, hoping to see a spirit in the shadows. But there was no hint of movement, ghostly or otherwise. A night-flying insect fluttered past his face, and he swatted at it languidly. The silence was broken by Tara shutting her door and walking to the back of the car.

"Help me get the stuff out if you've got nobody to talk to."

As they unloaded their cases, he heard a door opening. A gentle yellow light spilled from the main doorway, silhouetting a figure who waved.

"Hello!" a feminine voice said. "We were wondering if you were going to make it."

"We got snarled up in traffic," Craig replied.

The woman stepped out onto the flagstones of the courtyard. She was of average height with shoulder-length hair. With the light behind her, Craig couldn't make out her face.

"I'm Ellen. Can I help you with those? They look heavy. I suppose you've got a lot of cameras and stuff."

"Thanks!" Tara said.

Ellen Grant, despite her Scottish name, had a southern English accent not unlike a posh person in a movie. She also seemed to keep in shape, as she picked up two of their bags without difficulty and led the way inside, where they deposited their luggage in an impressive hallway. Craig peered up at faded battle flags and regimental shields, interspersed with portraits of stern-looking men in various historic uniforms.

"It's a bit old-fashioned, isn't it?" Ellen said. "Could I confirm your ID, by the way? Just the email confirming your booking is fine."

As Tara took out her phone, Craig got his first good look at the castle's manager. She was a pretty woman of about fifty, he guessed, with brown hair and gray-green eyes. Her face, slightly flushed by exertion, showed laughter lines. She wore a T-shirt and jeans with old sneakers.

"It's very attractive," he said. "I mean, the castle is attractive, in an old-world kind of way."

Tara gave him a wink and dumped her flight bag onto his toes.

"Yeah, it's cool. We can get a lot of great B-roll, I'm sure."

After checking their booking, Ellen gestured toward a door labelled LOUNGE, which stood half-open. Inside was a well-furnished room with a fireplace, unlit on this summer night.

"Would you like something to eat before I show you to your rooms? We have sandwiches and some homemade fruitcake. There's also tea and coffee."

"That would be great!" Tara said.

Craig followed the women into the lounge. There were more portraits, and some landscape paintings featuring stags and other wild animals. A large mirror hung above the mantelpiece. Craig checked his reflection and saw a pale, skinny guy with disheveled hair and badly wrinkled clothes. Tara was already taking a seat on a small sofa, looking hungrily at a table laden with sandwiches and cakes.

Someone else was in the room. They were unseen for now, but Craig could hear a sound that might have been sobbing or half-stifled laughter. He looked around, wishing he could check behind the sofa or the three overstuffed armchairs.

"Craig?"

Ellen was looking quizzical.

"Sorry?"

"Tea or coffee?" she repeated.

"Oh. Tea, I guess," he replied. "Don't need a caffeine boost right now."

Ellen smiled warmly.

"Two teas, then! Right, I'll just be two ticks," she said.

Craig watched her walk briskly away. Tara cleared her throat ostentatiously.

"What?" he asked.

"If we were an item, I think we'd be having a talk tonight," she said, smiling mischievously.

Craig felt himself blush.

"Don't be ridiculous. And I can hear a ghost nearby."

The sound faded even as he spoke the words, and he cursed himself for giving away the game.

"Is it still around?" Tara asked, unpinning her brooch and glancing around.

"I can't hear it anymore," he said, sitting down heavily beside her. "I went and blabbed. By morning, every ghost in Scotland will know a seer's arrived."

CHAPTER 22

A CONFESSION

"Can't be helped," Tara said, scrutinizing a small sandwich. "Word was going to get out sooner or later. Hmm, this is... egg mayo. Could be worse."

Craig checked the food and opted for a BLT, which was passable. The manager returned with a teapot and cups on a tray. Instead of leaning over to set it down, she bent at the knee. Craig said nothing, but his expression must have conveyed some surprise.

"Yes, I always do the Bunny Bounce," Ellen said cheerfully. "A legacy of my shameful past! I used to waitress at the Playboy Club in London. It was a good way to earn some extra money when I was a student."

A vision of Ellen in a Playboy bunny costume forced itself into Craig's mind. He visualized what might happen if she bent forward in such an outfit. He blushed again. After Ellen had gone, Tara jabbed what remained of her sandwich at him.

"Let's not mix business with pleasure, you dog!"

"Oh, stop messing!" he protested. "I'm not interested... I mean, she's way older than me... not that that should matter, but... see, it's unfair... oh, just shut up!"

He chomped on his ham and cheese sandwich. Tara, smiling slyly, poured two cups of steaming tea that emitted a pleasant fragrance.

"Earl Grey," she remarked and switched to a faux cutesy voice. "I guess she broke out the good stuff for her hunky American guest."

"Just stop!" Craig insisted, trying not to sound genuinely whiny this time.

"Ironic, though," Tara persisted. "We drove all this way in a Kuga, and now…"

"Stop; she'll hear you!" he hissed.

Tara changed the subject, and they finalized sleeping arrangements for the Red Chamber. Craig would check the place for ghosts, and if he found none, they would take steps to protect the bed. This would involve salt and iron filings to form a basic barrier, plus some basic rituals. They were tired but agreed they had to stay awake for another hour or so for these precautions.

"No defense is perfect," Tara said, "but given that no attacks seem to occur outside of the 12th, we should be okay for tonight and tomorrow. If you stretch your definition of 'okay' quite a bit."

Ellen reappeared after about ten minutes and asked them how things were. Things, the Americans agreed, were fine. The manager sat in a chair opposite them, and her outgoing expression changed to serious, even somber. Craig's instincts told him things were about to become less than fine.

"I have a confession to make," Ellen said. "I screwed up your room booking. I'd like to blame the computer or something, but I'm afraid it was just a silly mistake on my part. I double-booked the room in the tower. The one that's supposed to be haunted. So, I'm afraid you're in a different room, but it is a very nice one!"

For the first time since he'd arrived in the UK, Craig was genuinely pissed.

"But we… it was arranged a while ago," he said. "And nobody told us there was a problem, so…"

"Yeah," Tara put in. "We paid for that room."

Ellen raised her hands in a placatory gesture.

"I know, I know. It was only today when the other couple turned up that I realized."

"What other couple?" Tara snapped.

"They got here hours ago," Ellen explained. "And, of course, they had the email confirming their booking. So I had no choice but to put them in the tower room."

An argument ensued, with Craig wanting to play the role of peacemaker but too pissed to do it well. It was a fait accompli. Somebody was already in the Red Chamber and would be there for a week. Ellen, by way of compensation, offered them a more expensive accommodation at no extra cost.

"It's the Royal Suite," she explained. "King James IV of Scotland slept in it. It's by far the best room in the place! We often hold weddings here, and it's the one used by the happy couple."

Craig and Tara exchanged glances.

"What do you think?" Tara asked, still clearly disgruntled. "We rough it in the bridal suite?"

"Guess we have no choice," Craig said. "Would it be possible for us to at least film in the Red Chamber on the 12th?"

Ellen looked slightly relieved but still unhappy.

"You'll have to ask the other couple," she said, shifting slightly on her chair. "I did explain the situation to them."

That was a carefully worded answer, and Craig wondered if they'd get to see inside the room at all. Another thing struck him.

"Why don't you call it the Red Chamber?" he asked. "All the local history websites call it that, but you don't. Surely, it's a selling point?"

Ellen looked more uncomfortable.

"To be honest, there was a big debate when the current laird started taking guests. Some of the locals felt the room should be kept locked. Others poo-pooed the idea of a curse. But…"

Ellen leaned forward and lowered her voice.

"Some of the staff have heard things. And a few guests claim to have had chills, seen shadows, that kind of thing. Now and again, some guests have booked the room and then refused to stay in it. It apparently has bad vibes. That said, most people experience nothing untoward."

"Have you?" Tara asked, taking out her phone. "And can we interview you about this?"

Ellen looked taken aback but then laughed nervously.

"I don't know about an interview. I've only had this job for a few months. I've had the sensation of being watched from time to time, but that might just be imagination. Small objects do seem to move around or get hidden away, only to reappear later. We've had trouble with the Wi-Fi and the power. But this is a remote location, and the wiring isn't new. So…"

Craig started talking about his ghost tours and added a few details about YouTubing which he hoped didn't sound asinine. He had done some research. Tara's mood improved as she joined in, adding a few telling details and mentioning the years she'd spent in England. The conversation gradually became amiable again. Ellen remained unwilling to be filmed, though. She looked on as Tara recorded a brief segment about the mix-up over their rooms. It had, at least, provided more content.

"Oh, I almost forgot!" Ellen exclaimed, jumping up. "I was in such a tizz, I didn't ask you to sign the register."

She hurried out and returned with a large book with a red leather cover. Craig produced a pen when Ellen realized she hadn't brought one. He took his time signing the book, adding his home city and the initials USA. Lingering over the task meant he could read the names above his. Two people had signed in earlier that day. One signature was a spidery scrawl, but the other was very clear.

Ramona Kleist, who gave her hometown as Stuttgart.

He passed the book to Tara, who spoke to Ellen as she added her signature.

"So, the other guests are German?"

"Well, continental," the manager replied. "I'm not sure about their nationality, but they do seem to speak English most of the time. Slightly odd, but presumably, it's the only common language they've got."

Ellen glanced at the doorway and then lowered her voice.

"They're a bit of an odd couple. He's much older than her, and… well, I shouldn't gossip. You'll see them at breakfast."

She retrieved the guest book, thanked them profusely, and asked if they would like to see their room.

"To the bridal suite!" Tara said, punching the air and jumping up.

Ellen led them past the reception desk, through an archway, and up a stone staircase. It was rather narrow, and Craig remarked on this.

"Yes," the manager said over her shoulder. "Much of the old castle survives, despite a fire and a lot of renovation. These narrow stairways were easier to defend."

"Guess so," Craig said.

He imagined men armed with swords and spears retreating upward, jabbing down at attackers. It would not be easy to take a castle like this. Assuming, of course, anyone could get past the moat and the walls in the first place.

The walls to either side were decorated with rosettes of swords arranged around circular shields. The shields were made of wood with a metal boss in the center and large metal studs. Craig lingered to study one more closely, taking out his phone to snap a photo. As he did so, a face emerged from the shield and leered at him. It was a young man's ghost, with a pale, thin face visible under an unruly mop of ginger hair.

"Oh, God," he muttered, reeling back.

CHAPTER 23

LANGUAGE BARRIER

The two women paused to look as he tottered for a moment and dropped his phone, which bounced down the stairway. The ghost laughed loudly and then said something quickly that Craig did not understand. The ghost's accent was thick, and the words were unfamiliar. The spittle flying from the spirit's mouth was also distracting. Then the apparition was gone, and Tara was holding Craig's arm as he regained his balance.

"You okay?"

"Yeah, guess it's just… I'm more tired than I thought," he said. "And these stairs are kind of steep."

"Yes, just take your time, guys," Ellen said. "I was racing ahead a bit, sorry!"

They resumed the climb as Craig rebuked himself for being startled by a spook. Of course, if he'd been prepared, he would have understood what the ghost said. A worrying thought struck him. He thought back to Zack, the student on the plane. Zack and Tara had talked about the huge range of local accents in the UK.

"Um, I guess people round here have a special… is it a dialect?" he said.

Ellen, who had just reached the top of the stairs, looked down at him curiously.

"Indeed they do," she said. "Some of the older folks are a bit hard to understand. Lowland Scots is not a distinct language, but it comes pretty close. Younger people speak more standard English, though. It's like everywhere, the old ways dying out, what with the internet and such."

"So I guess," Craig said slowly, "if I encounter any local ghosts from the Middle Ages, we'll struggle to have a conversation?"

"Well, yes, I suppose so," Ellen said cheerfully. "Now, this is your room. I think you'll like it!"

Ellen's description of the room's features passed him by. He'd never given a moment's thought to language. He'd encountered a few ghosts back home whose English had been poor, but he'd never struggled to comprehend them. This was an extra challenge he did not relish.

"What gives?" Tara asked as soon as Ellen had left. "Something's bugging you."

Craig told her.

"I might not be able to understand the ghosts here. They're not going to talk like characters in Braveheart or whatever."

He watched the realization dawn on Tara's face. She slapped a hand to her forehead and sat down heavily on the bed, which creaked slightly under her weight.

"Why didn't I think of that?" she moaned.

"We both should have," Craig said, pacing back and forth. "But maybe it's not so bad. The one who spoke to me might have been from Viking times or something. Hell, he might have been a Viking or a Celt or whatever."

Tara kicked off her shoes and lay on the bed.

"We can't be sure," she said quietly. "We need more data points. Let's think about this."

Craig decided to do something, anything, and started to unpack. This reminded him of the need to protect them. He got out salt and made a ring around the bed, following it up with iron filings. Meanwhile, Tara was researching Lowland Scots. It was the language in which the poetry of Robert Burns had been written. The name meant nothing to Craig.

"He wrote Auld Lang Syne," Tara explained.

Craig was only vaguely familiar with the song. Like many people on New Year's Eve, he just made vaguely musical noises if a case of Auld Lang Syne broke out. All he knew was the chorus. Tara, it turned out, was much the same.

"Burns wrote in the eighteenth century," she said, lying on her back and scrolling through menus. "Ah, here's one of his poems. Oh, God. Here, see what you make of this."

Craig sat on the bed and took the phone. The first two verses of Burns' poem did not fill him with optimism.

> *Ca' the yowes tae the knowes,*
> *Ca' them whar the heather grows,*
> *Ca' them whar the burnie rows,*
> *My bonnie dearie.*

> *Hark, the mavis' e'enin' sang,*
> *Soundin' Cluden's woods amang;*
> *Then a fauldin' let us gang,*
> *My bonnie dearie.*

There were more verses. Craig felt that "my bonnie dearie" was a nice sentiment, but Burns could've just written the rest in plain English.

"I guess with practice I might get along okay if the accent isn't too strong. I know some of those words, and I can guess at others from context…"

He trailed off. They didn't have much time for him to practice Lowland Scots or any other dialect. Tara took back her phone. Craig tried to think of a Plan B.

"Okay, maybe ghosts from more recent times could talk to earlier ghosts and act as translators."

Tara sat up and slapped him on the back.

"You're right. We need to stay positive. We've arrived, we will get into the Red Chamber, and you will contact the ghosts. And we'll get a good night's sleep. Let's get started on those incantations."

They sat side by side in the middle of the bed, reading the occult verses from Tara's phone. The words were less challenging than the Burns poem. They went through a series of Latin phrases Craig had studied earlier, along with their translation. Tara had explained that using Latin rather than plain English enhanced the effect. It required more mental discipline and focused the mind on the ritual. Craig suspected that it also added a touch of class, but perhaps that amounted to the same thing.

The core of the ritual was a repeated invocation to mysterious higher powers. The idea was that good beings would help ward off evil.

"Protegat et servet me, ab omni malo defendat me."

Which meant roughly, "Protect and keep me, defend me from all evil."

After making this plea three times, they bowed their heads, eyes closed. Craig imagined a heavenly being looking down and deciding to give them a break. It seemed unlikely, but so was their mission. The silence became uncomfortable, and he had to speak.

"What do we do now? Because I'm tired, but I don't think I can get to sleep. I'll just worry."

Tara said nothing for a few seconds. Then she raised her head and looked him in the eye.

"What if the couple in the Red Chamber is in danger? What if one of them—or both—has done military service or something? A lot of Europeans get drafted in peacetime."

Craig groaned slightly. Another complication. But there was a simple solution.

"We tell them the truth. We've looked into the legend, and we have a theory. Warriors are killed in that room. It fits our role as YouTubers who hunt ghosts."

"Yeah," Tara said, "I guess that's the right thing to do. We'll see them at breakfast, I guess."

The thought of food made Craig wish he hadn't left one of the uninspiring sandwiches, let alone a couple of cakes, behind. He looked at the selection of uninspiring cookies next to the inevitable kettle and pulled an energy bar out of his sports bag.

"You want one?" he asked.

"Nah, I'm good," Tara said, getting up. "I'm gonna take a shower and get some shuteye."

Her phone chimed while she was in the bathroom. Craig knew by now that the particular note signified that an email had arrived. When Tara came back into the bedroom, she was wearing a robe and a towel wrapped around her hair. Her pale skin was flushed pink. He found himself briefly fascinated by her toes. Realizing he was on the brink of being a perv once more, he went to shower.

She was waiting for him when he was done, dressed in baggy sweatpants and an oversized T-shirt that bore the slogan, "Astrophysics is Fine in Theory." She was smiling and holding up her phone.

"Shane's on his way," she said. "Arriving in a day or two. He's had some problems, but he paid the problem-creators back with interest. That's the impression I get."

Craig's spirits rose and then sank a little.

"That's great. Maybe he can think of a solution to the dialect issue."

Tara's expression became smug.

"I asked him about that and—for a wonder—he replied right away. Said it's no problem. He can understand any language a ghost might speak."

Craig blinked, astonished.

"Yeah, it's like a superpower, right?" Tara laughed. "Reinforcements are on the way."

CHAPTER 24

FROM THE NEW WORLD

Craig woke to find Tara sprawled across most of the bed. For a smallish woman, she covered a wide area. Craig had gradually retreated during the night and was now precariously close to the edge of the slightly lumpy mattress. Nothing good or bad had happened during the night.

Tara mumbled something in her sleep and turned over, settling again with her back to him. He moved a little closer, wondering what she was dreaming about. She spoke again, and he thought she said "Marcus".

As far as Craig knew, Marcus Mortlake was still incommunicado. He had half-hoped and half-feared that the English professor would get in touch with Tara. An expert occultist who knew the territory would be a great ally. But Tara had not mentioned her mentor on the journey from London. It was reasonable to assume that Mortlake was still off the radar.

Craig got up, stretched, and realized a moment too late that he had scuffed a gap in the salt barrier that encircled the bed. He froze, expecting a manifestation. The gibbering spirit that had startled him on the stairs might still be around. But seconds ticked by, and he sensed no uncanny presence. He swept his hands across the scattered salt to fill the gap.

"Hey, something wrong?"

Tara was lying on her side, her hair covering most of her face. One green eye gazed blearily at him.

"I kicked some salt away and thought there might be an attack, but there's nothing."

Tara got out of bed and stretched luxuriously.

"Maybe the word got out," she said. "We don't take shit from ghosts."

Craig found that view optimistic, but it might have been true. He walked to a window as Tara went into the bathroom and looked out onto the courtyard. The Royal Suite was impressive in daylight, and he felt better about their situation. So far, they had survived attacks and attained their first goal. When Shane arrived, they would have an effective fighter and ghost-seer. According to Tara, he could make it by the 11th. Tomorrow afternoon was cutting it close, but Craig chose to be optimistic. The fact that Shane was joining them at all was a triumph. The guy hated traveling outside the U.S.

"So, you're the man from the New World."

The voice was low, with a distinct Scottish accent. Craig turned around to see a small, slender woman about three feet away. The outline of the bed and the doorway was faintly visible through her. She wore an old-fashioned floor-length dress and a plaid shawl over her shoulders. Her strikingly red hair had partly escaped from a frilled cap. In her arms, she held a bundle that stirred slightly. A swaddled child, Craig guessed.

"Um, yeah, I guess I am," he said.

The woman looked down at her baby.

"The New World. Perhaps we should have gone there while there was still time. But we had nae siller."

No silver, he realized after a moment. *No money for the voyage. So… maybe she died in the eighteenth century.*

Tara emerged from the bathroom and paused, mouthing a question. Craig nodded but added a thumbs-up. This spirit did not seem like a threat.

"I am here seeking the cursed sword of the Laird McIvor," he said loudly. "Do you know where it is?"

The ghost continued to look down at the little bundle. The infant made a whimpering noise, and its mother swayed and crooned a wordless tune. Craig repeated his question, lowering his voice, afraid of upsetting the baby even more. The woman gave no sign that she had heard him. Tara, calculating the woman's position from Craig's line of sight, moved quietly to the bed and took a dagger from under her pillow.

The ghost ended her song suddenly and looked at Craig again. She smiled and held out the bundle to him.

"Will you take him from me, good sir? Will you take my poor wee bairn to the New World when you return there? Some say you have that power. I do not know if it is true, but you have a kind, honest face."

As she spoke, her face became even paler and started to gleam with perspiration. Patches of red glowed on her cheeks. She shivered and stooped a little. Craig did not need to ask what had ended her life, and that of her child. A fever of some kind, one of the dozens of infections that claimed so many in the old days. Just another statistic to be mulled over by historians and economists. Yet, here before him was the truth. A human life that had ended so prematurely and unjustly.

"I… I can't take him in my arms, I'm afraid," he said, searching for a way to tell her what he could do. "But I will take you both to… to a new world."

The woman's eyes grew huge.

"Oh, my lord, that would be…"

Her words were lost in a fit of coughing, and she fell to her knees. Craig knelt too, reaching out with his mind and focusing on the task. But he could not help wondering how many times this woman had pleaded with strangers, most of whom could not see or hear her.

Moving her on proved far more difficult than he expected. Craig struggled to focus. His power seemed weak, attenuated somehow. The woman, her head bowed, continued to shed tears that dampened the infant's swaddling. Craig caught a glimpse of a tiny face, its eyes screwed up. A baby on the verge of a meltdown. Again, he struggled against the distraction.

The vortex opened.

The ghost was aware of the change and looked up, her eyes wide and mouth agape. The infant began to bawl weakly, as a sick child would. The vortex was different this time. The whirlpool of light was a gentle pinkish glow that expanded to reveal a landscape of rolling hills and lush forests. A small cottage of pale gray stone stood by a stream, with smoke emerging from a chimney.

A humble vision of paradise, he thought. *Her New World.*

A ray of sunlight shone through the gap in reality. The baby stopped crying and gazed up, his face illuminated with golden radiance. The woman stood, holding up her infant to the strange, new sun. A timeless moment ensued during which Craig experienced every fleeting memory of a life that had ended more than three centuries ago. The intensity of the feeling hit him so hard that he gasped. He heard someone calling his name but could not reply.

The golden light vanished.

He was in the fetal position, his heart racing, and his limbs numb with a throbbing pain. Everything around him seemed unreal, a hollow sham, compared to the life he had just relived. A familiar face filled with anxiety. A pretty young woman was kneeling by him, repeating his name. A large knife lay on the carpet close to her right hand. He wondered why she would have a knife. Perhaps trouble was brewing.

Then, his memories flooded back.

"Tara?" he croaked.

"Jeez, what did it do to you?"

She helped him get up and hobble to a chair.

"I'll be all right," he said, trying to sound as if he believed it. "I guess I just need to recharge my batteries."

He explained what had happened as best he could. Tara listened while making him a cup of coffee.

"It's instant, but at least it's got caffeine in it," she said as she handed him the cup.

He gulped down the hot liquid, nearly scorching his throat. It helped offset the lethargy that replaced the discomfort he'd felt after the portal closed. He had never felt this drained. It seemed that, while his power had evolved, it had also become more demanding, and maybe trickier to control.

"You lived someone else's life in maybe a second," Tara observed after he described what had happened. "Guess that's going to be a problem. This gift of yours is turning into a curse. Or more of a curse than it was. I guess this means we should keep you away from cities from now on. These European cultures go way back, and that means you'll be knee-deep in lost souls. Too much suffering for you to handle."

CHAPTER 25
BEST MEAL OF THE DAY

They talked over the problem of Craig's new power for a couple more minutes, before Tara suggested breakfast. This made more sense than contemplating forces neither of them could understand or control. As they descended to the foyer, Craig half-expected the jabbering ghost to reappear, but the spirit didn't manifest itself. Instead, they met Ellen Grant at the foot of the steep, winding staircase. When Ellen saw Craig, she couldn't help reacting with shock, even covering her mouth with her hand for a moment.

"Oh, dear lord! You didn't sleep well at all! Was it the room?"

"No, I'm just jetlagged," he replied. "I guess it caught up with me all at once."

"Well, let me recommend a full Scottish breakfast," the manager said. "Our cook called in sick today, so I'm on kitchen duty."

"Sounds good," Craig said.

"Two, please!" chimed in Tara, raising her hand as if in class.

"Two it is! Nothing like a hearty breakfast to set you up for the day!" Ellen said.

She hesitated and then lowered her voice.

"Kurt and Ramona are in there," she said, jerking her head toward the dining room, "but I don't think they'd be very agreeable to you approaching them over breakfast. Some people are a little grumpy in the morning."

She walked off briskly toward a door marked KITCHEN. Craig

took a moment to grasp that she was talking about the people in the Red Chamber. Ellen turned as she opened the kitchen door and gave him a wink, and then she was gone.

"You seem to be recovering nicely," Tara said sotto voce. "Must be something in this country air. Or could it be the influence of a shapely if somewhat mature posterior?"

"Aw, come off it," he said, as they resumed their walk to the dining room. He was still thinking of a smart rejoinder when two guests came into view. Tara saw them at the same time and gave a low whistle.

"Wow. Kurt and Ramona, I guess."

The two people getting toast from a buffet table looked like Olympic weightlifters. Ramona had short, cropped blonde hair that looked dyed. Kurt was hairless, with massive shoulders and huge biceps that bulked out of his athleisure gear. Both sported abundant tattoos in various languages. Craig thought he recognized German, Latin, and what might have been Chinese characters.

The pair moved ponderously across the smallish dining room like tanks. They nodded curtly, unsmiling, when they caught sight of the Americans and then went to a corner table. So far as Craig could tell, the Germans were having orange juice, lightly done toast, and oatmeal. He wondered if they had brought protein shakes and supplements to consume in their room. They looked the type.

Wouldn't want to tangle with them, he thought as he poured two cups of coffee and waited for the toast to brown. *Mercenaries seeking the sword would look like that.*

The only other guests offered a massive contrast: a middle-aged British couple who was chatting cheerfully over plates bearing the remnants of a hearty breakfast. They waved Craig and Tara over to a table adjacent to theirs and introduced themselves as Alfie and Carol Bright.

"Bright by name," Alfie said, then chortled, "but not by nature, I'm afraid."

"He's thick as two short planks, but I still love him," Carol chimed in. "So, what brings you to this part of the world?"

From their accents, Craig guessed they were from the south of England, which the couple quickly confirmed. Craig had never heard of Orpington and said so.

"It's quite nice in a boring sort of way," Carol explained.

"Just like me," Alfie added.

Craig laughed a little uncertainly. He knew British humor could be ironic, self-deprecating, or sometimes just plain filthy. The Brights seemed typical in that they used weak jokes as a shield to avoid getting too serious about any particular subject. He caught a sour glance from Kurt as he and Ramona stood. The bodybuilders strode past the Brights' table, speaking in low voices and avoiding eye contact.

"See you later!" Carol called.

There was no response from the two bulky figures passing out of the room.

"They seem fun," Tara remarked.

"Oh, they're the Kleists. They're not so bad," Alfie said. "Just very focused, you know? Intense. And you've got to hand it to the Germans; they're very efficient. Good planners—get it right the first time, and all that. We went to Germany last year, didn't we, love?"

The conversation became an account of a cruise up the river Rhine, with the inevitable display of pictures on Alfie's phone. Craig learned that the Brights had seen many fine castles and cathedrals and enjoyed a lot of beer and sausage. Craig was relieved when Ellen Grant arrived with a heavily laden plate that she set in front of him. The full Scottish breakfast was remarkably like the full English, only the sausage had somehow become a square of cooked meat. There was also something Ellen referred to as "tattie scones".

"Mashed potato flatbread," Alfie explained helpfully. "Goes nicely with the baked beans."

"I'll be back with yours in two shakes," Ellen said to Tara before turning back to Craig. "You eat up. You need to get your strength back, young man."

Craig tucked into his meal while Tara did her best to get some information from the Brights. When Tara mentioned the mix-up over their room, the couple was full of sympathy. Alfie said that "somebody should be held accountable," as if a crime had been committed. Carol tutted at him and said complaining never got you anywhere, but that they should get a discount.

"But why," Carol asked eventually. "Why do you want to sleep in a room where such horrible murders happened?"

Tara repeated their cover story, and Alfie instantly began searching online for their content. The Brights asked lots of questions about YouTubing and paranormal investigation. Carol was slightly more probing, while Alfie continued to take every opportunity to crack weak jokes. They seemed harmless enough to Craig, but perhaps that was the idea. The Germans stood out like very large sore thumbs. The Brights were the kind of people you might meet anywhere.

Or maybe they're all innocent, Craigh thought. *Maybe we're the only ones on this quest.*

"Of course," Carol said, "you'll want to visit the haunted chapel."

"Haunted?"

Craig felt a mixture of hope and trepidation.

"Oh yes," Alfie chimed in. "They say the ghosts of the Red Laird's victims can sometimes be seen, wafting around, weeping and wailing. Not very often, of course. If ghosts appeared all the time, it would devalue the currency, wouldn't it?"

Craig thought of his life since early childhood but forced himself to smile at the cheerful Englishman.

"Yeah, I guess it would."

"Maybe we could go to the chapel after breakfast, honey," Tara said.

Craig stared at her. She was putting on a sweeter voice than usual, almost a parody of feminine adoration. He felt sure the Brights would see that their alleged relationship was fake, but Carol seemed to find them both adorable.

"Ah, love's young dream!" Carol said. "Remember when we were like that, Alfie?"

"I don't think I was ever that good-looking," Alfie said, surprising Craig.

This prompted more banter between the Brights. Tara's breakfast arrived, and the Americans focused on chowing down. As the conversation flagged, the English couple got up to leave.

"See you later, alligator!" Carol said.

"Not if they see us first," Alfie quipped.

After the couple was out of earshot, Tara spoke.

"There's many a true word spoken in jest."

Craig was about to agree when he caught sight of a figure outside the French window of the dining room. It was an old man, shabby and unshaven, with a mane of tangled gray hair. He was staring at the Americans.

"What is it?" Tara asked, turning to look.

"A ghost, maybe, but…"

Craig fell silent as Ellen returned to ask if everything was all right. The old man walked slowly out of sight. Craig decided that this was as good a time as any to lean into their YouTube ghost-hunting image.

"I think I might have just seen a ghost," he told Ellen and then described the old guy.

Ellen's eyes widened, and she laughed.

"Oh, no," she said, "that's Hamish. He's a gardener and an odd-job man. A bit scruffy, I agree, but he's harmless. And alive, as far as I know. I mean, if he wasn't, we wouldn't be paying him, right?"

CHAPTER 26
WOE TO THE VANQUISHED

They went for a walk after breakfast. Seen in daylight, Castle McIvor was slightly less impressive than at night. There was a dilapidated air about the structure, especially the older parts that dated from medieval times. The tower with the Red Chamber looked solid enough, though. Signs of newer stonework were here and there.

"They refurbished the tower," he remarked.

"Money spinner," Tara said. "A haunted bedchamber is free publicity. Still pisses me off that Ellen double-booked it."

After the Hamish incident, Craig felt they had established themselves as harmless eccentrics in Ellen's eyes. This might not be a bad thing if they had to do things of a questionable nature—like sneak into the Red Chamber.

Tara gave a faint smile but said nothing. They walked out of the courtyard through the imposing gate, and Craig stopped short of the drawbridge.

"Maybe we should go back and get the AV gear," he suggested.

"Nah," Tara replied, taking out her phone. "We can film each other and upload some inane stuff for now. It's the first day. We're finding our feet, scoping out the terrain, et cetera."

Craig nodded but did not say anything.

"I guess that's the chapel," Tara said, pointing. "Looks picturesque, like a folly."

Craig had no idea what a folly was. Tara explained that old-time aristocrats often had fake ruins built on their estates to enhance the view.

"Ruins or maybe Greek temples, that kind of thing," she added. "But I guess the chapel is the genuine article. According to Wikipedia, there was a church on this site for more than a thousand years. It fell into disrepair around 1600."

Craig's mind was again boggled. He had not given sufficient thought to the depth of time he was supposed to explore. In America, the population had not been very great before the eighteen hundreds, and the number of ancient ghosts was accordingly low. The term "Old World" took on a new meaning here.

Could be worse, he thought. *We could be in Egypt. Or China.*

They crossed the drawbridge and followed the gravel driveway until a footpath branched off. It led to the chapel but circled a low mound that lay between the castle and the ruins. It was the burial site from which the sword had been excavated. In their preliminary discussions, they had talked about exploring it to see if some clues could be gleaned. Tara asked if Craig was still up for that.

"Now is as good a time as any, I guess," he said.

After a few minutes, they turned off the path and trudged toward the mound. Craig kept an eye out for ghosts but saw nothing decisive. A figure appeared around the corner of the castle, but using the phone camera magnification, it was identified as Hamish. Then, they caught sight of two sturdy figures in gray and black jogging ponderously down the driveway toward the road. Kurt and Ramona Kleist. They weren't very fast but had achieved a lumbering momentum that seemed unstoppable to Craig.

"Wonder where they're going," Tara mused.

"Probably going to wrestle a cow and eat it," he suggested.

They reached the base of the mound, which was about four feet high, thirty feet long, and fifteen across. It was overgrown with wild grass and a few straggling bushes that lay almost flat. Craig wondered how windy the area got in the winter months. Very, he guessed.

"Anything?" Tara asked, still filming with her phone.

"No, I don't sense anything," he said, feeling self-conscious. "The spirit of anyone buried here probably moved on a long time ago."

"Let's climb up," she suggested.

From the top of the mound, they got a better view of the chapel ruins. They consisted of three walls and the sad stump of a long-ago-collapsed tower. No trace of a roof remained. He used his phone to take a panoramic shot of the landscape, including Tara, who gave a "peace" sign.

"We're in Bonny Scotland!" she proclaimed. "We were hoping Craig would sense something about this burial mound that might date back to Celtic times, like two thousand years plus. But so far nothing; right, honey?"

Craig began to reply, but the sky changed. The morning sun was suddenly robbed of light, and all color was leached of its pale blue and turned black. He was standing, not on a mound of earth but on a vast plain. The ground, what he could see of it, seemed to consist of dark, gritty soil or sand. He thought of volcanic ash, an idea reinforced by a reddish glow in the distance. Apart from the crimson light, the world was dark. No moon or stars were visible, nor any hint of trees, buildings, or anything that might have relieved the grim vista.

A moment later, Craig realized he was not alone.

Someone advanced toward him, silhouetted against the hellish glow. The figure had long hair that fell around its shoulders. It raised a sword over its head and charged, screaming something incomprehensible. Craig flung up an arm to protect himself, but the phantom did not seem to see him, charging past so that he saw it faintly illuminated by the reddish glow. The man was naked, his pale skin decorated in what looked like elaborate tattoos. Along with the sword, the running man had a roughly rectangular shield strapped to his left arm.

Other figures moved across the plain, too. They seemed to be converging, slowing down, and forming a loose line of men. There might have been hundreds, but it was hard to tell in the poor light. Craig got a sense of urgency and heard more shouting, chanting, and a rhythmic thumping noise. The beating of metal against wood. Sword against shield.

Then, Craig's attention was caught by something in the distance. Moving across the dead land was an object that he could not clearly make out. It might have been a machine, as it glinted dully. The size was impossible to gauge without a point of reference. It might have been a hundred yards away or several miles.

The plain, he now saw, was not entirely featureless but had a few low ridges and shallow basins. The mysterious gleaming thing had crested a ridge and was now descending. The new angle let him see that it was not one object but several squares arranged like a checkerboard. Craig recalled an old movie he had seen on TV and realized what was advancing.

An image flashed into his mind. It was bizarre, out of place, and not part of this world but somehow connected to it. Some kind of sculpture, a statue, but it also seemed alive. Then, somebody clutched his arm. The black, starless sky was replaced by regular daylight, and he blinked down at Tara's anxious face.

"What happened? Did you see something?"

"Yeah. I just got a flashback to the Old World."

He looked down at the grass, still damp with dew.

"The guy who was buried here? I think he fought the Romans."

Tara had never seen *Spartacus*, but she took Craig's word about a Roman legion advancing in a checkerboard formation. It was, he opined, something about one block supporting the others and being able to better maneuver.

"But that's kind of irrelevant," he said, realizing he had strayed out of his comfort zone. "The point is, the Romans stopped by, and there was a battle. Maybe it was the same legion I saw farther south, near York."

They descended from the mound and then looked back at it.

"It's not surprising," Tara said thoughtfully. "The Romans advanced a lot farther north than Hadrian's Wall. Hell, they built another one in the middle of Scotland, but I think they had to abandon it."

They resumed their walk toward the chapel. Tara had stopped filming and was surfing the web on her phone. Craig used his phone to shoot a few minutes of video as they approached the ruins. No ghosts were in evidence on the screen, but when he stopped filming and looked up, he saw vague forms moving in the shadows cast by the morning sun.

"Tara…" he said quietly.

CHAPTER 27

THE CHAPEL OF UNREST

"You see anything?"

Tara put her phone away. They both know that this might be a serious confrontation. They had come equipped with a dagger each, plus containers of iron filings. Tara had her hand on the hilt of her weapon, which was concealed in a special loop sewn into her jacket.

"Not sure," he said. "They seem skittish, not threatening. Erratic."

The way the ghosts moved reminded Craig of the discarnates of Grendon Mill. Those ghosts had been spirits wrenched from their tormented bodies by sorcery. Perhaps the same thing had been practiced in Europe? Craig told himself to be calmer and not see threats where none might be. Still, he slowed his pace as they approached the chapel.

"This place gets a lot of tourists," Tara said quietly. "If the ghosts were a threat beyond the Red Chamber once a year…"

There had, Craig recalled, been nothing online about the chapel ruins as a place of danger. This didn't quite reassure him. Word had somehow gotten around. He had experienced a similar phenomenon back home. He knew ghosts talked to other ghosts, and they could sometimes be a gossipy bunch, but his reputation had spread here very quickly, and he was not on his home turf.

"Okay," he said. "Let's see if I can communicate."

He picked his way over some tumbled stones in the undergrowth and entered the church. Weeds sprouted from between flagstones and almost covered the altar. Now he was inside, Craig became acutely aware of the tower and walls. The official guide to the castle said the building was "relatively safe", but guests ventured into the ruins at their own risk.

"Are they doing anything?" Tara asked.

"No," he said, focusing on the ghosts. "Well, they're drifting back and forth behind the altar. Near the doorway to the tower."

Even as he spoke, he lost sight of one shadowy form as it retreated into the darkness at the base of the tower. It was followed by two others. A couple of ghosts, still hard to discern, lingered. They were shy. Unusually so, by Craig's standards. He wondered if that, too, was connected to the depth of history here. Ghosts that encountered people frequently over centuries might well become averse to human contact. They could feel despair and regret at witnessing the antics of the living. He'd met a few in the States and they were invariably from way back.

"I could approach one," he said half to himself.

"Be careful," Tara urged. "I got your back."

He walked slowly toward the altar. A bird that had been hiding in the undergrowth flew up with a shocking clatter of wings. His heart racing, Craig stopped, distracted. The bird, a large crow or maybe a raven, was perched on the wall to his left. It cawed with what seemed like derision. When he looked at the tower entrance again, only one ghost was visible. It was almost transparent, barely visible in the deep shadow.

Craig held out a hand.

"I can see you," he said softly. "I can help you move on if you want to leave this world."

The spirit stayed motionless for a few heartbeats. Then, it began to drift toward him, becoming more opaque as it did so. He could see now that the ghost was that of a short man in a dark robe fastened around his waist with a cord. His face was round, with dark button-like eyes, and a small, pursed mouth. There was just a thin sprinkling of hair around the shaven crown of his head.

A monk, Craig thought. *A man of learning. But will he speak words I can understand?*

"Hello, you lovebirds!"

Carol Bright's voice echoed from the ivy-clad walls, far more startling than the bird's antics. Craig cursed under his breath. The monk was still visible but had retreated. The figure vanished into the shadows a moment later.

"Oh, Carol, we've interrupted some ghost hunting!"

Alfie's voice was jocular, a fake rebuke.

Tara had already turned a bright smile onto the couple, who had walked up behind the Americans. Craig forced himself to greet them warmly. A germ of an idea was forming in his mind as he parried questions about spooks.

"To be honest," he said when the Brights were both silent for a second, "I sensed a presence. A medieval monk. I saw him right there."

He pointed to the space behind the altar. The Brights looked skeptical but didn't cast doubt on the claim. Craig elaborated on the ghost's appearance but didn't mention moving the monk on. That was something he would not reveal yet, if at all. But convincing the other guests that the chapel was haunted might be useful.

"Thing is," Alfie said, smiling indulgently, "if you could talk to a medieval monk, you probably wouldn't understand them. They'd either be speaking the local dialect or perhaps French. That was the language of the ruling elite, you know?"

"Fascinating," Craig said. "But maybe, after hanging around all these centuries, some of the more intellectual ghosts might have picked up a few handy English phrases? You never know."

Carol giggled.

"You talk as if ghosts are always floating around, watching us. That would be shocking. Imagine if you were in the shower or… well, you know."

"Spending a penny?" Alfie suggested and got a shove from his spouse in response.

"She means taking a whiz," Tara translated for Craig. "And maybe ghosts are watching us all the time. I mean, if every generation leaves ghosts behind, this country must be kind of crammed with spooks, right?"

Carol laughed uncertainly. Alfie nudged her in the ribs and winked at the Americans.

"She'll be peeing with the light on for months now!"

Craig decided to head off more British humor by asking what the Brights were going to do that day. The answer was the usual mashup of banter and information. But Craig gleaned they were going to a nearby town called Berwick-upon-Tweed to check out a gastropub that served real ale and something called Toad in the Hole. He decided not to ask for clarification.

"I think," he said, "we'll go and get some of our gear and get some more footage."

The Brights still looked skeptical but made encouraging noises. Craig waited for them to turn and walk away, and then caught Tara's eye and made a gesture of pinching something between finger and thumb. She mouthed the word "Really?" He mouthed "Yeah!" and gestured emphatically at the retreating couple. Tara rolled her eyes but went along with the plan.

Craig watched as she furrowed her brow. Her power was, she'd told him, limited in range but would reach farther than her physical limbs. The Brights were about ten feet away when Alfie suddenly yelped and jumped a couple of inches. Carol stopped dead and looked at him in puzzlement, glancing around.

"You okay?" Craig asked.

"Somebody pinched my bum!" Alfie blurted out.

The Brights looked at the Americans. Craig hoped his expression of innocence was as good as Tara's.

"Maybe it was a ghost," he said. "Poltergeists are kind of playful sometimes."

"Yeah," Tara added, "and you asked for it by doubting that this chapel is haunted."

Alfie's expression remained suspicious, but Carol giggled and gave him one of her nudges.

"Serves you right! We'd better get going or the spook might pinch you somewhere else."

CHAPTER 28

JUST LACHLAN

"You want to contact that ghost again?" Tara asked after the Brights were out of earshot.

"Might be worth a try."

Craig hesitated. Something about their conversation with the Brights bothered him.

"Is it weird to you that Alfie knew all that about medieval ghosts speaking French?"

Tara looked toward the couple, who was halfway to the main gate.

"I don't know," she said. "If he spent some time online looking up stuff about the castle…"

"Guess I'm just paranoid," Craig said. "Okay, let's see if I can speak to him."

He walked slowly over to the altar and peered into the doorway. The tower was a ruined stump, but the remaining walls still blocked almost all the light. It was hard to tell if the slight flickers of movement were ghosts or just shadows of foliage stirred by the breeze.

"Hello? Is there anybody there?"

A whisper came from the gloom. Then, the moon-faced monk appeared, more substantial than before. Craig filled in Tara on the ghost's return.

"He look friendly?" she asked.

"Not unfriendly," Craig replied.

The monk spoke.

"I am a friend to the virtuous, and I avoid the evildoer."

The English was crystal clear, with an accent very much like Ellen Grant's. Craig blinked.

"Okay, that's good to know."

The monk moved closer, into the daylight, until he was just a couple of feet from Craig. He might have been a living man in fancy dress. Craig smiled, and the monk smiled back.

"How do you do?"

"I do well enough for a dead man," the monk said, smiling for the first time. "Who do I have the honor of addressing?"

Craig introduced himself and Tara. The monk introduced himself as Lachlan of Beamish. He explained that he had learned over the centuries to modify his speech to suit the times but rarely got the chance to use it. That, Craig thought, explained why he sounded a little old-fashioned and stiff.

"Yes," Lachlan said when Craig put this to him. "A short conversation with a passing seer every few years is… slim pickings? Is that the right term?"

When Craig explained this to Tara, she came up with an interesting question.

"Ask him why he doesn't just haunt the castle and listen in on convos there all the time?"

Lachlan's eyes widened.

"Dead or alive, I am still a man of God! Others may spy and pry, but I refrain from such Peeping Tom antics. I converse only with such wayfarers who come here, my proper domain. Having said that, I do sometimes pop in to watch the TV, but a lot of it is incomprehensible."

Trying to keep his face straight, Craig relayed this to Tara. She sensibly changed the subject. Facing a little to the left of Lachlan, she asked if he knew where to find the sword of Laird Angus. Lachlan did not look pleased by the question.

"You seek a cursed weapon!" he said, raising an admonitory finger. "Nothing good will come of it."

"Yeah," Craig said, feeling suddenly weary. "You're not just going to tell us where it is and then we can go?"

The monk crossed his arms and shook his head firmly.

"Would it help if I helped you move on?" Craig asked, trying not to sound wheedling.

The monk smiled slightly.

"I tarry on Earth as a punishment for my sins in life," he said. "The Lord God will decide when I am fit to be removed to a better place... or a worse one."

Craig couldn't stop from asking if Lachlan's sins had been so bad. The guy seemed nice enough. The monk's face darkened, and he looked down at the weeds and rubble.

"I doubted my faith," he said. "I despaired of God in the time of the plague. I asked myself if all the things I had learned from my first years as a penniless orphan were mere... myths and legends. That was my sin. My punishment seems apt. Every moment that passes offers me more proof of the supernatural."

Craig felt sorry for the monk and wished he could offer some consolation. He relayed the conversation to Tara, then asked another question.

"But, you were a good man in other ways? I mean, you did good deeds, were kind, worked hard? Stuff like that?"

Lachlan shrugged.

"We were bound by our vows to do such things. I believe you would call it 'the bare minimum'? No, my faith faltered, and I must pay the price now."

After Craig had relayed this to Tara, she again spoke in

Lachlan's general direction.

"Can I suggest something? Destiny brought his man…" she pointed to Craig. "Destiny brought him here. How do you know he is not God's instrument? Perhaps he can move you on, but not before you share some information with us. How about that?"

Lachlan looked sniffy but not wholly skeptical at the suggestion.

"Let me ponder this matter," he said. "I am troubled in my soul. I would not want to make a reckless decision."

Craig couldn't help groaning.

"Can you make it sooner rather than later? We're kind of on the clock here."

But Lachlan was already fading into the shadows, his cherubic face blurring into a pale oval, then vanishing. Wind stirred the greenery at the base of the ruined tower.

"He didn't buy it?" Tara asked.

"He's thinking it over," Craig said, and turned to see they were being watched.

"Just as well, given your exhaustion," Tara said, then she, too, realized they were not alone.

The German couple loomed in the gap where the main door had once stood. They were stony-faced as usual. Kurt spoke.

"Good morning."

It was not said in a friendly tone, but at least it was an opener.

"Morning!" Craig replied. "We just had a little ghostly encounter."

Ramona gave a little snorting laugh.

"Surely you do not believe in such things?" she said. "Ghosts are stories for children."

"That's a pity," Tara said, "because we think you're in danger from the ghost of the Red Chamber."

For the first time, Kurt looked uncertain. Ramona, however,

simply sneered.

"Because some people died in our room, we should be afraid? Statistically, any bedroom will see a certain number of unusual deaths if enough time passes."

Craig couldn't help thinking that it was a very German way of looking at things. Cool, efficient, and logically irrefutable. But still dangerously wrongheaded.

"Look," he said, "we think everyone who died was a warrior or a fighter in some sense. Did either of you serve in the military?"

This time both Kurt and Ramona looked unsure of themselves.

"That is none of your business," the German woman said.

"No, but it might be the ghost's business," Craig said. "Look at the facts!"

Craig went on, outlining the evidence that the ghost killed those it saw as invading enemies. As he spoke, he saw the Kleists' uncertainty change to stubborn dismissal. Kurt's lip curled with contempt as Craig suggested that they leave the room on the fateful anniversary.

"This is all nonsense," Ramona said, making a dismissive gesture with one brawny arm. "We do not fear phantoms. Tell your stories to someone else."

Craig and Tara watched the musclebound couple set off back toward the castle.

"Well, we told them," Tara remarked. "At least they have a day to think about it."

CHAPTER 29

A BEFUDDLING MESSAGE

They decided to go back to their room to get camera gear. On their way up the winding staircase, the ghost that had startled Craig made another appearance. It seemed that the spirit enjoyed leaping out at him. This time, Craig was ready.

"Where is the Red Laird's sword?" he asked.

The youth's expression changed from merriment to confusion and then fear. The ghost mumbled something and vanished. Craig felt immense frustration, and cursed. He explained to Tara what had just happened.

"The thing is," he said, "the guy might have been telling me what I wanted to know. I wish Shane was here."

"Yeah," Tara agreed as they resumed their climb to the second floor. "And he might come in handy if Kurt and Ramona are after the sword."

When they were going through their gear, Craig noticed that one of the small containers of iron filings was half-empty. He had used one full container to create the barrier around the bed the previous night. Or had he? He doubted his memory and asked Tara if she knew.

"You used up one completely," she said. "I saw it."

Craig held the container up to the light. There was a trace of a fingerprint. Or maybe a thumbprint, as it was quite large. He thought of the Germans again.

"If Kurt and Ramona searched the room while we were at

breakfast, they might have opened a vial to find out what was in it. And, being kind of ham-fisted, one of them might have dropped some. They couldn't pick up the filings, but maybe they smudged them into the carpet?"

Tara pondered that, then found an objection.

"If they're in the same line of work as we are, surely, they'd know about iron?"

"So," Craig said, "maybe they're not like us at all. Maybe they honestly don't believe in the paranormal. But if so, why book the Red Chamber? Unless they think there's something of value in there. Some clue, maybe?"

"We need to search their room," Tara said. "Turnabout is fair play."

Craig asked if she knew how to pick locks.

"Oh yeah," she said, tapping her head. "That was one of the first things I learned when I decided to do this crazy gig on a professional basis. All we need is some way to make sure they are out of their room for a while."

"If they go jogging again, it should give us at least half an hour."

They discussed it some more while selecting what equipment to use. Craig would be on camera as he was already known for his ghost tours. He was mic'd up as they recorded some footage of the inside of the room before going out into the corridor. Craig kept up a commentary on the castle, the legend, and their experience at the chapel ruins. He downplayed the sword, focusing instead on the mysterious deaths in the Red Chamber.

As they reached the foyer of the castle, Tara's phone pinged. She apologized, stopped filming, and glanced at the screen. Then, she froze.

"Shane?" Craig asked.

No, Tara mouthed, glancing around in case they were

overheard. Then, she held up the phone for him to see. The sender was Marcus.

The great Professor Mortlake, Craig thought. *At last, some help.*

"Hello, hello. You two lovebirds engaged in surveillance?"

Carol Bright was sitting on a sofa facing the reception desk. Her husband was nowhere to be seen. Craig silently gave thanks that he would be spared the Brights' wearisome double act.

"Just getting some B-reel," he replied. "Would you like to give us an interview?"

Carol's face changed from amiable curiosity to panic, but just for a moment. She shook her head firmly and held up a hand.

"Not without my face on! I look a terrible sight without makeup."

Craig wasn't quite sure how to respond to that, so he just smiled and hoped it seemed sincere. Carol got up and hurried away, saying something about lunch. It seemed a little early. Watching the woman vanish out the front door, Tara summed up Craig's view.

"She doesn't seem to want her face online, which is odd. Women that age are normally all over Facebook."

"Maybe she doesn't want anyone to know they're here," Craig suggested. "We know they like taking holiday pictures. They must have photographed themselves in front of every castle on the Rhine."

Tara shrugged.

"Maybe we're overthinking it. There's a difference between taking selfies on vacation and appearing in someone else's vlog."

They stepped outside into the castle courtyard. Carol was nowhere around, nor was anyone else. Craig double-checked to make sure nobody could overhear them from an open window, ushering Tara to the center of the courtyard. Then he asked her about the message from Mortlake.

"Oh, yeah. It's a bit weird."

She held up the phone and tapped her thumb on the screen. The email opened to reveal a terse message. Just two letters: IX.

"Roman numerals, I assume?" Craig asked.

"Yeah, nine," Tara said. "I guess he didn't have time to send anything else. I wish I could just talk to him. As it is, I guess we decipher the clue. But first, let's go see your pal the dead monk again. See if he's changed his mind."

Filming almost at random, they retraced their steps toward the chapel. They didn't stray toward the mound this time, choosing instead to linger for a few moments to shoot some footage. Craig thought again of the sparse facts about the ancient burial site. Angus McIvor had ordered the mound excavated, seized the sword that was found, and gone crazy. Amid the general mayhem and confusion that followed, the original aim of the earl had been forgotten. Treasure.

"I wonder if they missed something?" Craig said.

"One thing we can be sure of," Tara said, "is that the priest didn't put the sword back in the grave. It's almost certainly inside the castle. But maybe…"

She nodded toward the chapel.

"A priest might think consecrated ground would be a good way to neutralize a possessed object."

"That sounds way too easy," Craig said a little gloomily. "But let's see if Lachlan is going to cooperate."

Before they reached the chapel, however, a small red Nissan turned into the courtyard. Craig saw that the left front fender was dented and the paintwork scuffed. The car swerved and came to a halt a couple of yards away. The driver's window slid down, and Shane Ryan looked out at his two startled associates.

"These right-hand-drive cars are the worst," he said. "Had a little trouble getting through that front gate."

Shane got out and walked around the front of the Nissan to inspect the damage.

"The other guy just got a scrape anyhow," he went on. "No real damage. Think you could wrangle it so Stark pays for this?"

Tara was staring open-mouthed. Craig laughed, mostly from relief.

"I thought you weren't coming until tomorrow?" he asked.

"Basic stuff," Shane said, kicking the Nissan's tire. "If comms might be intercepted by the enemy, send misleading data. I don't trust electronics, and that's before we consider the possibility of psychic powers and all that jazz."

He walked around the back of the Nissan, opened the trunk, and lifted out a large black bag.

"So," he said, setting the bag down, "where's this sword?"

CHAPTER 30
ANCIENT HISTORY

Craig helped Shane carry his stuff inside. Shane had no weapons, but as Craig had observed, the other man's fists had served him well so far. Ellen Grant seemed quite taken with Shane as she checked him in and showed him to his room. Craig fought jealousy and made a point of ignoring Tara's smirk.

Shane's room was on the ground floor with a window facing the castle gate. It was small, but the newcomer pronounced it fine.

"I've stayed in much worse places."

Ellen asked them what would like to order for lunch. There was a brief discussion.

"I hope you enjoy your stay," she added while looking at Craig. "We aim to give our guests total satisfaction."

After the manager left, the conversation quickly turned to more serious matters as Shane had a series of questions. He was intrigued by what they had found. Also, Craig's enhanced but exhausting power gave him pause for thought.

"Could be," Shane mused, "that it's the presence of so many ghosts. Best lay off all that 'moving on' stuff unless it's vital. Now, what were you saying about this ghost that just kind of jabbers at you?"

They led Shane to the spiral staircase, and he walked ahead of Craig, with Tara behind. Predictably, the red-haired youth appeared, his head protruding from the wall. His manic grin turned to surprise when Shane reached out and grabbed him by the throat.

"Okay, pal," Shane said, "let's hear it. Who are you, and why are you messing around up here?"

The ghost jabbered some more. Shane responded in regular English at first but after half a minute or so was speaking what was evidently the ghost's dialect. Craig thought he heard the words "bird" and "barrow", but he wasn't sure. Interestingly, Shane seemed to become less annoyed with the ghost during their dialogue. He let the ghost go and the young confused visage disappeared back into the stone wall.

"Interesting," Shane said, turning to face his companions. "That guy was around when everything happened."

"Maybe we should take this outside, then?" Tara suggested.

They walked downstairs again, and Shane waited until they had passed through the gate and over the moat before giving his account.

"That boy was confused, to put it mildly," he began. "Not right in the head, they'd have said in the old days. Challenged, I guess we'd call it now. So his memories are kind of jangled, and he seems to spend most of his time wandering around, spying on the living, and making friends with other ghosts."

"I'm guessing the other dead folks aren't too keen on him?" Craig asked.

Shane shrugged.

"Old-time prejudices. Whatever the reason, he's lonely. He was keen to talk, but like I said, it came out in no particular order. There was something about a golden bird…"

"Right," Craig said. "It was linked to Celtic warriors heading out to fight the Romans. Didn't those guys carry eagles? That was their symbol, right?"

"Nine!" Tara exclaimed. "I knew there was something."

She hadn't mentioned Mortlake's message to Shane yet, so she recapped that. Shane listened carefully and then gestured to the burial mound.

"The Romans carried golden eagles with silver wings as their standards," he said. "If I remember right, those eagles were gods. A deity for each legion. They had priests, prayers, offerings, the whole nine yards. And when one was taken in battle, it was like the regiment died. Was there a Ninth Legion around these parts?"

Tara was already Googling.

"Yes!" she proclaimed triumphantly. "The Ninth Legion, called Hispana because it was formed in Spain under Caesar Augustus. It was sent to Britannia, as it was then, and according to some reports, it set out from Eboracum—that's York—to suppress a rebellion in the north of the Roman province. No record of the Ninth Legion exists after the year 120, just before Hadrian's Wall was built."

The three of them paused to look around. Craig felt he was seeing the pleasant, sunlit landscape with new eyes. Here, or somewhere nearby, a battle had been fought. He recalled his vision of the checkerboard formation advancing over the hills, and the pale warriors with blue-dyed skin racing toward them. How had such a disciplined force been defeated?

He put that question to Shane.

"Hey, it happens all the time. Your equipment and training might be great, but if you don't know the territory and your CO gets too confident, chances are, you're toast. And the guy defending his wife and kids has all the motivation. I guess the Ninth came up against some clever guerilla tactics or maybe just blundered into an ambush. Bit of both, maybe."

"Back in those days, all of this would have been forest," Tara said with a wave that took in most of the landscape. "They cut down the trees centuries ago so the landowners could graze sheep."

Shane nodded sagely.

"Yeah, that tracks. It would have been great ambush country.

Rolling hills and dense forest. And that mound—what the boy called the 'barrow'—is where the tribal leader was buried with his treasure. And his sword. My guess is he died in battle, and his thoughts were just full of rage against the Romans, the intruders. Could be other factors at work, but that's the heart of it."

They walked on toward the chapel, passing the mound.

"You think the Eagle of the Ninth is still buried in there?" Craig asked. "I mean, we'd know if anyone else had found it, right?"

Tara pointed out that somebody might have sneakily dug up any treasure from the mound during the last few centuries. It was once common to melt down precious metals regardless of their cultural value.

"They found an Anglo-Saxon crown back in the sixteen hundreds down on the coast of Norfolk I think," she added. "That was melted down right away. One of the great treasures of England, lost forever. A Roman Eagle would be even more valuable to archaeologists, but the chances of it surviving must be pretty close to zero."

They talked on, focusing now on the Red Chamber and what to do about the Germans. Shane's view, predictably, was that the Kleists had been warned, and if anything happened to them, that was just tough. Seeing Craig's response, Shane pointed out that for all they knew, the couple were hired thugs of the worst sort.

"If they're just innocent tourists," he added, "they have nothing to worry about, right? I know you want to believe we're the good guys, and I guess we kind of are, but that doesn't mean we have to protect people who might turn out to be murderers."

Craig saw the logic in that, he just wished they knew more about the other guests. It seemed unlikely that Kurt and Ramona were regular tourists. A thought occurred to him. He stepped over the remains of a wall and walked up to the altar. Dark shadows, now familiar, swirled restlessly.

"Lachlan?" Craig called. "Can you do us a favor? It will help determine if some people are bad and deserve punishment, so I'm guessing it's right up your alley."

CHAPTER 31
FAKING IT FOR REALSIES

"It was amazing!"

Craig feigned moderate excitement as Tara showed Ellen the video. They were standing on the threshold of the dining room. Along with the manager, a young waitress viewed the footage they'd recorded at the chapel.

"This is the best evidence for a haunting I've seen!" Ellen enthused. "And to see it in the chapel rather than the castle. Maybe that's where previous ghost hunters went wrong?"

"It is remarkable," Tara agreed. "You see, Lachlan is a medieval monk who's lingering on the earthly plane to atone for his sins; right, Craig? And he manifested these phenomena to prove to skeptics that he is real."

Lachlan had not manifested anything. And none of the other chapel ghosts would talk to Craig, but the team had anticipated this. Tara had used her psychokinetic power to lift a small rock and hurl it against the altar. Then she had done it again, this time with an empty Coke can. Then Craig and Tara had produced convincing oohs and aahs at their prearranged stunts.

"Hello, hello, what's going on? Having a conference, are we?"

Alfie and Carol Bright appeared from the stairwell and came over. They were impressed by the video and were soon indulging in some of their customary banter. Then the Kleists came in through the front door and stood scowling at the cluster of people blocking their way to the dining room.

"This is fascinating stuff!" Alfie called to them. "Our young American friends have got some remarkable footage of a poultrygeist."

"Poltergeist!"

Carol nudged him in the ribs.

The German couple reluctantly came forward, and Tara held up her phone.

"We just need to do some editing and stuff before we upload it," Craig explained. "I guess when this goes public, the estate will be swarming with sightseers. It'll be good for business; right, Ellen? Better make some more of those great sandwiches."

The manager agreed, but Craig was more interested in the Kleists' reaction. They were not quite stony-faced as they gazed at the video, and they exchanged a glance as soon as he mentioned crowds of visitors.

"It is very interesting," Ramona said, looking at Craig shrewdly. "This ghost, you can see it?"

"I have that ability," he said. "Call it a curse or a blessing, but I can see ghosts and talk to them. Lachlan had a lot of interesting things to say about stuff buried in the chapel. It seems there's some kind of treasure there, but he wasn't too clear about the details. Guess I'll find out more after lunch."

The Germans looked at each other again before Kurt spoke to Ellen.

"We would like to eat now."

The group moved into the dining room and took up the tables they'd occupied at breakfast. Shane, who'd been silently observing until now, found himself in conversation with the Brights. His cover story was straightforward and almost true. He told the British couple he was an old friend of Tara and Craig and would sometimes assist in filming. He did his best to seem amiable and interested in chit chat.

"You can see them, too?" Carol asked.

"Yeah, most of the time," Shane said. "There's a red-headed boy on the stairs who seems to like jumping out at people. He's harmless, I guess, but didn't you sense a presence? Sometimes, if a ghost touches you, there's a cold sensation."

The Brights immediately launched into a discussion and soon concluded that, yes, they had felt a distinct chill going up to bed last night.

"And you said it was a draft blowing up my skirt," Carol chided her husband.

"Well, if you wear those skimpy undies, you're bound to get a chilly bum," Alfie retorted.

All the while, Craig had noticed the Kleists observing the Americans, especially Shane. The dynamic had shifted; it was now three against two. However, he felt the Germans still had the advantage. Craig had fought the cultists at Grendon Mill, but they had been a gang of small-town murderers, not skilled close-quarter fighters. Either of the Kleists looked like they could tear a normal-sized person limb from limb without breaking a sweat.

"So, what's next on the agenda?" Craig asked during a lull in the Brights' chatter.

Tara took her cue.

"I guess I'll be editing most of the afternoon," she said. "Of course, you two could go and have another word with Lachlan."

"Yeah," Shane chimed in, "it's worth a try."

"Ooh, can we come?" Carol asked.

"It's a free country," Shane replied.

"The more, the merrier," Craig added.

Ellen Grant appeared with a couple of desserts, followed by the waitress.

"Hey," Craig said, "if we find some buried treasure, do we get any of it? Or does it all belong to the King or whatever?"

The manager placed a plate of eclairs in front of Tara and then straightened up and frowned.

"Well, I think any precious metals belong to the crown, but the finder gets a share of the value. Of course, anything *really* old is bound to be wanted by a Scottish National Museum up in Edinburgh. That could get complicated pretty quickly!"

The Brights naturally had an opinion on this.

"Very unfair if these young people have put in the work, talking to ghosts and all!"

"Yes," Alfie said, "Tell you what. If we find anything after lunch, we'll just stick it up our jumpers and not tell anyone; right, chaps?"

Light-hearted suggestions flew back and forth. Craig took out his phone and used the camera to look over his shoulder at the Germans. They were deep in conversation, hunched forward so as not to be overheard by anyone passing their table.

When lunch was over, the team collected their gear and set off for the chapel with the Brights in tow. As they passed the burial mound, Craig looked back and saw two substantial figures following close behind and heaved an inward sigh of relief. Whatever their motives, the Kleists had fallen for it. They would be away from the Red Chamber for a while.

The tricky part was yet to come.

CHAPTER 32

CRYING IN THE CHAPEL

The little group clustered around the two Americans. Shane, still maintaining his cover as the couple's friend, set up a GoPro camera while Craig talked enthusiastically about Brother Lachlan and filmed the altar and tower on his phone. The ghost was present, looking with interest at the disparate visitors. Alfie and Carol chattered loudly, occasionally including Ellen and the other staff. The Kleists stood slightly apart from the rest with their trademark scowls, observing closely but saying nothing.

"Okay," Craig said, "I am sensing a presence."

The ghostly monk standing three feet away raised an eyebrow at this. Craig tried not to laugh.

"Yes," Craig went on, "Lachlan is here. I think he is going to… move among you?"

He swung his phone around, not tracking the ghost's actual movement. Lachlan walked past Craig, right up to Carol Bright, and reached out a plump, white finger. He barely brushed the woman's cheek. But Carol shrieked and slapped a hand to her face.

"Something touched me!" she yelped, stumbling backward and almost falling. "Bloody hell, it was like ice! Icy fingers!"

There was a suitably impressed response from Ellen and the staff, while Alfie put a comforting arm around his spouse. The German couple glanced at each other, then looked at Craig.

"I think… yes, he is saying something," Craig said with his eyes closed, trying to look and sound like a medium on a TV show.

"Lachlan, do you have a message for anyone here?"

Lachlan did, as they had rehearsed it all beforehand. Craig opened his eyes and stared at Ellen Grant.

"He says—I don't understand this, and I'm sorry if it's embarrassing—he says Hamish took your lingerie."

Ellen's eyes widened and then she laughed heartily, almost doubling over with mirth. Others joined in, and even Shane cracked a smile.

"So that makes sense?" Craig asked.

"Oh, my God!" cried the manager as she recovered. "I left them drying by the window. Oh dear."

The ghost laid his fingers lightly on Ellen's shoulder and she gave a shriek.

"Lachlan says that Hamish wears them, so you probably wouldn't want them back."

"Oh God."

Ellen was bright red now. The others, even the Kleists, looked fascinated. Craig had been right to ask Lachlan to come up with some information that was funny as well as factual. Brits liked jokes about knickers and bras; it was that simple. Shane had been skeptical, but Craig had successfully argued that humor was a better way to engage an audience than dire warnings.

Craig carried on with the routine for another couple of minutes, Shane joining in to point to roughly where the ghost was. This led to more shrieks and nervous fidgeting, especially from the young waitress. Craig had learned that the girl was from Romania, and she seemed genuinely scared, not joining in the Brits' laughter. In fact, she seemed close to tears and was clinging to Ellen's arm. The manager did her best to reassure the younger woman.

"It's all right, love. The ghost isn't going to hurt anyone."

"One among us is afraid," Craig said, looking at Lachlan.

"Please, brother, do you have some words of comfort for her?"

"An angel stands at her shoulder," Lachlan replied. "It is radiant with goodness. It shields the maiden with one of its shining pinions. Would that I had such a protector in my earthly toils. Do you not see it?"

Craig wondered if Lachlan was making this up, though it seemed out of character. He'd not previously considered that there were some supernatural beings he could not see. Craig shook his head and relayed the monk's words. The girl seemed reassured but was still wide-eyed and skittish, and he had no time to think about it now, as his phone began to ring.

"Hello?"

"Get over here; I've jimmied the lock," came Tara's voice.

"Really?" Craig said, turning to look at the guests and staff. "You found something on the video we took yesterday? Okay; I'll be right over. Shane can handle things here. See you in five."

This was the crucial moment. The plan was for Craig to offer release to the ghost of the Red Chamber. If it was the long-dead Celtic warrior, it might have had its fill of killing. He could not, of course, speak a long-dead language, but they had contrived a workaround. If this was not the case, Craig was, in theory, immune to ghostly attack. It was a theory he hoped would not be put to the test. Apart from anything else, he was not immune to pain from any source, ghostly or otherwise.

They had discussed whether Shane should be involved. Tara had taken the view that a ghost seer who was also a warrior might trigger a violent response from the phantom of the Red Chamber.

The other worry was that the Kleists might become suspicious and return to their room. If they did, Tara could use her power to lock the door, assuming she had sufficient warning. If the Germans caught them in flagrante, however, things might get messy.

Or rather, messier.

CHAPTER 33

THE RED CHAMBER

Halfway up the stairs, Craig met the red-haired ghost boy. This time, instead of leaping out to startle him, the apparition was just standing and waiting. Shane's intervention had set him straight on a few things. The boy smiled broadly at Craig and then pointed out the stairs and cocked his head to one side.

"Yes," Craig said, nodding vigorously. "Now is the time."

The ghost bounded up the spiral staircase two at a time. They passed the second-floor door and then arrived at the landing outside the Red Chamber. Tara was waiting, the door open, but she opted to stay outside. There were too many unknowns for her to enter the room alone.

"Hey!" she said.

Craig did not reply. Tara was not alone, though she didn't know it. A tall, broad-shouldered man stood by the doorway to the bedchamber, a room where he had slept many centuries ago. Angus McIvor, the Red Laird, looked down at Craig. For all his ferocious appearance, the man cut a tragic figure. Craig had seen many unhappy ghosts in his time. It was hardly unusual for the dead to be depressed, but there was a depth of misery in the laird's eyes that Craig had never seen.

"There are two ghosts here," he told Tara.

She followed his gaze and stepped away from the laird.

"Do not fear me, lass. Oh, do not fear me."

McIvor's voice was deep but gentle, and heavy with melancholy.

Once, Craig knew, the laird had led men into battle for his king and country. Now, he seemed worn out and shadowy. Craig could make out hints of door frame and stonework through the ghost. This was a man who had endured centuries of suffering, a ghost haunted by its past in a way no living man could imagine. McIvor had committed abominable sins in a mad rage. Craig could only admire the fact that the laird had remained more or less sane in all the centuries that followed.

"It's okay," he told Tara.

The laird looked squarely at Craig and shook his head.

"I doubt ye can win over the wild one, lad. He listens to no one and is merciless in his rage. I know. I felt his spirit flow through me like a river of brimstone, like wildfire in a forest. All-consuming. Remorseless."

Craig straightened up and hoped he looked resolute.

"I am the first who can send him onward to a better place. Doesn't he want to join his ancestors? Isn't he tired of killing after all these years?"

The laird gave a massive shrug, his enormous shoulders moving under faded plaid wrappings.

"Mayhap he is. It has been a goodly while since I last saw him. Yet, we are still bound by blood rage and blood guilt, and I sense that he is not ready to yield to any man."

Craig felt the laird's intuition had to be respected, but he also had a duty to give it his best shot.

"Let me try," he said quietly and walked inside.

The room was very tidy, as he'd expected. There was no sign of any possessions other than a gym bag carefully placed on a stool under the widescreen TV. There was a slight odor of sweat in the air, and he imagined Kurt and Ramona going through their morning calisthenics half-naked, or maybe fully unclothed.

Focus, he told himself.

There was certainly a presence here. It was powerful, and it radiated a dull, throbbing anger. Hostility toward all intruders. That was the distinct impression that bled over into Craig's mind. He had crossed the threshold and was now the focus of attention. But where was that attention coming from?

He waited for the observer to make a move, but nothing happened. The room was silent.

"Come in, guys," he said quietly. "He knows we're here, but he doesn't seem too riled up at the moment."

Tara walked in and stood to Craig's left. She did not hold any weapons in case they prompted a hostile response, but Craig knew she'd slipped daggers down the back of her jeans, concealing them with her oversized sweatshirt. The two ghosts moved politely around the Americans and paused by the king-sized bed. The red-haired boy giggled and pointed at the window. No, Craig realized, at a spot just below the window.

"Talk to him for me," Craig urged. "Explain who I am, and—"

He stopped as a wave of intense cold flooded over him. Tara gasped at the same time.

"He knows who and what you are," the laird said.

"Ask him," Craig said. The cold was not letting up. He could see his breath, and Tara was hugging herself and shivering.

"Ask him if he wants to move on."

The laird shook his head and then spoke to the red-headed youth. The boy nodded emphatically and spoke a few words in what Craig presumed was an old Celtic dialect. The cold intensified for a moment, then eased. A new voice sounded in Craig's mind. It was faint, not distant but whispering urgently. The ghost youth listened intently and then spoke to the laird.

For the first time, McIvor looked slightly hopeful.

"The warrior asks if you have the strength to send him to meet his ancestors. Do you?"

Craig thought of how drained he had been when he'd moved on the woman and her baby. How much more energy might be drawn from him if he helped the spirit of the sword? The only way to find out was to do it. With luck, it would work. If things went wrong, Tara would intervene and attack the ghost. This opportunity might not come again.

"I can do it," he said. "Tell him that this is my destiny, and his."

The wave of coldness returned, but only for a moment. Then shadows shifted by the window. The flickering shadows grew darker, merging to cover a patch of the deep red carpet, and expanding to become a three-dimensional shape.

And then a brawny arm wrapped itself around Craig's throat.

CHAPTER 34

CLOSE QUARTERS

"What are you doing in our room?"

Ramona Kleist let go and spun him around to face her, then resumed her grip on his windpipe. Her massive left hand was balled into a fist and raised to smash into his face. Craig felt a strong urge to make peaceable noises, but with his throat nearly being crushed, he couldn't have replied even if he'd wanted to. Out of the corner of his eye, he saw Kurt holding Tara by both arms as she writhed and cursed.

"This is a criminal offense," Kurt said. "We will report this to the polizei."

"I doubt that," Tara said, still making futile attempts to free herself. "We know what you're here for."

It was a random shot, but it struck home. Craig felt Ramona freeze and relax her steely grip slightly. He tried to break free, but a second later, she had wrestled him to the floor and was sitting astride him. He was almost crushed under a mass of solid muscle and bone.

"You are the criminals!" she shouted, smacking him hard across the face. "Admit that you broke into our room to steal!"

A horrifying thought struck Craig. Was this the first time in centuries that anyone had fought in this room?

"Don't you understand… you're in danger… by doing this?"

Tara instantly grasped his meaning.

"Yeah," she shouted. "Stop fighting! We can talk it through!"

Kurt was not in the mood to listen. Instead, he lifted Tara and flung her onto the bed. As she fell, one of her daggers came loose and slid across the covers. The blade gleamed dully in the sunlight. After a moment's silence, the Kleists became enraged.

"You came to kill us and take ze treasure!" Ramona said, now sitting astride Craig, holding him down with one hand and raising the other in a fist again.

"Treasure?" Craig said before what felt like a wrecking ball hit him in the face.

Stunned, he lost consciousness for a moment, then heard Tara yelling at Kurt to keep away. A dagger whirled through the air, spinning end over end before vanishing from Craig's field of view. Ramona hesitated, her fist raised, staring toward the bed. Craig felt hot blood gushing from his nose and gagged as it ran into his mouth. Then, a pain far more intense than the bodybuilder's punch pierced him.

It felt like a red-hot blade plunging into his chest. His body spasmed, and he screamed, the sound like a high-pitched gargle as blood sputtered into the air and fell back onto his face and into his eyes. He blinked. His vision was now blurred, and the room's white ceiling seemed stained pink. But Craig could still see that Ramona Kleist was frozen in the act of smashing her fist into his face a second time.

Behind her loomed a shadowy form like a three-dimensional shadow. Flashes of fire swirled within the figure of darkness. Two glowing green eyes peered down from an otherwise featureless face. The ghost was leaning forward, and as Craig stared, transfixed, it straightened up and pulled a blade from Ramona Kleist's broad back. The sword was just visible against the darker form of its wielder. The weapon gleamed with traces of red, blue, and purple radiance.

The woman collapsed onto Craig like a sack of cement. He had no doubt she was dead. The sword thrust must have gone straight through her heart. He heard Shane's voice now, and Ellen Grant's, mixing with those of Kurt and Tara. Craig felt he was suffocating and began to drum his hands and feet on the floor for attention. As if by some miracle the lifeless mass was lifted, and he saw Shane looking down anxiously while Kurt heaved his partner onto the bed.

"Call an ambulance!" the German cried.

Ellen Grant already had her phone out. Craig sat up and Tara started helping him to his feet. Then, everything seemed to happen at once. Alfie Bright appeared in the doorway behind Ellen and grabbed her phone. She protested, and he sprayed her in the face with something from a small black container. The manager screamed and put her hands to her face, making choking sounds.

"What the hell?" Tara demanded.

At the same moment, Kurt said something in German that showed he was just as surprised.

Carol Bright appeared and pointed a gun at Tara.

"Don't try anything, love. I'm faster on the trigger than you are with your psychokinetic parlor tricks. Anybody causes trouble, I put a bullet right between her eyes. You wouldn't want that, would you?"

Shane, standing between Craig and the doorway, fell into a crouch. Alfie took a step back.

"Don't be stupid," the Englishman said, tossing aside the spray canister and taking out a gun of his own. "Now everything's under control."

Kurt stared wildly at the newcomers. He had one knee on the bed and his fingers pressed to Ramona's sturdy neck as he felt for a pulse. He gave a sudden, discordant yell and leaped to his feet. Alfie looked alarmed, but Carol barely reacted.

"Shoot him, then," she said calmly.

Alfie aimed and fired. From his vantage point, Craig saw the bullet leave the back of the German's head with a spray of blood, bone fragments, and brain tissue. Kurt pitched forward and hit the floor with a crash.

"Jesus Christ," Craig murmured.

"Now you know we mean business, folks," Carol said, her voice eerily calm. "But there's no need for any more nonsense. You can concoct a story about who killed who and why when we're gone. Two bodies; maybe it was a lover's tiff."

"Yes," Alfie chimed in. "No need for a massacre, not here of all places."

"That's right," Carol said, almost resuming her cheerful persona. "Just tell us where the sword is, and we'll be off."

There was a very awkward silence.

Carol leveled her gun at Craig while Alfie took her place with Tara.

"You seem to be the lynchpin of your team. If you don't know, and they don't know, you'll soon be joining Kurt."

CHAPTER 35

THE PHANTOM OF THE SWORD

"I'll count down from five," Carol said. "Make it nice and dramatic for you."

Craig was fascinated by the fact that the woman who threatened to shoot him in the head was wearing a comical T-shirt. It was pink and decorated with a cartoon cat and the slogan "Kitten Mom". It seemed a suitably absurd end to a life he'd never quite gotten a handle on.

"Five."

He wondered why the ghost of the sword had not intervened. It seemed like a clear-cut case. Then, he saw a shadow moving behind Carol and Alfie, sliding along the wall. No one could be casting that shadow.

"Four."

The shadow began to form into a vaguely man-like shape. Two green eyes flickered open. A blade about three feet long appeared, gleaming in unnatural light.

"Three."

Carol cocked the pistol. Craig had seen this done in dozens of movies and TV shows, but somehow, the click seemed far louder. He wondered if he would hear the shot. He realized an instant later that he had begun to pray.

"Two."

The ghost raised its dark phantom sword behind Carol's head. Craig closed his eyes and braced for a death—preferably not his own. He found no more prayers, only an odd sense of completion. In the aftermath of his death, there would be a moment of confusion, and he imagined Shane and Tara would sort things out between them.

"One."

No sound came. Then, he heard someone muttering words rapidly, words Craig could not catch. Shane swore. Craig opened his eyes to see Carol lowering the gun. Behind her, Alfie was no longer aiming his gun at Tara. Instead, he was holding up a small, round object that looked to be a statuette carved from greenish stone. Alfie was speaking, his voice low and urgent. The ghost of the sword was frozen in place, its weapon raised to strike at Carol but seemingly unable to deliver the blow.

"We're not bloody idiots, you know," Carol said. "We came prepared. Now don't interfere, and we'll be done in two ticks. I'd rather not shoot anyone else. It makes everything more complicated."

She gestured at Craig with her gun, barked more orders, and he moved over to stand alongside the others. Ellen Grant was sitting on the bed, her eyes red, still weeping profusely. Tara and Shane were kneeling with their hands on their heads.

Alfie, meanwhile, had thrust the miniature idol into the shadowy form of the ghost. It lost its definition and flung out sparks of red and purple. Craig heard a howl of agony, faint but still heart-rending. A soul in torment.

"Stop, you're hurting…"

He faltered, and Carol laughed.

"Tenderhearted lad, aren't you? How many people has that bugger killed? You're almost as daft as those two."

She nodded at the bodies of Kurt and Ramona.

"All they wanted was the Eagle of the Ninth," Carol went on.

"Pathetic. It must have been melted down ages ago. But they helped distract you clowns, so they served their purpose. A few clues planted online got them over here at the right time."

Craig struggled to process this information, at the same time realizing that Carol was bragging, delighted by her cleverness. Alfie continued his chanting, moving the stone idol in a figure eight inside the writhing outline of the long-dead warrior. Craig wondered what he was doing. Then, he saw dark filaments growing from the trapped ghost. They lashed back and forth like the tentacles of a strange sea creature in its death throes before reaching across the room. The threads of intense shadow flailed around near the window, before settling on the great slab of stone that formed the sill.

"Easy," Carol said.

She gestured again with the gun.

"Okay, you lot. Get over there and lift it."

"Hurry," Alfie said, sounding strained. "The bastard's stronger than I thought."

"You heard the man!" Carol shouted. "Lift it."

It makes sense, Craig thought. *The priest who took the sword had only a boy to help him. Maybe he intended the hiding place to be temporary.*

It was pointless to speculate, and he found it hard to think with a gun pointed at him. It became apparent that the four of them couldn't all get a grip on the granite slab. Shane sourly pointed out that it was mortared in position anyway. Carol wasn't fazed by that. She ordered Ellen Grant to get something to chip away at the mortar.

"And make it snappy!"

Ellen ran outside. The room was silent but for Alfie's chanting. The sword ghost was still twisting and thrashing as Alfie moved the statuette through its insubstantial form. Then, another ghost appeared: the ghost of Angus McIvor. Craig wondered if Carol was a seer or if only Alfie had that power. There was no tell that the woman saw McIvor as he approached Craig. Alfie was looking the other way.

Shane's eyes flickered briefly and then refocused on Carol's gun. He saw an opportunity looming, but there was no obvious way to let Tara know. The laird stood close to Craig and looked sadly at the Brights and their captive. Then he leaned closer to Craig, presumably afraid that Alfie might overhear.

McIvor asked a question. Craig nodded briefly. Carol looked puzzled for a moment and seemed about to speak. But then Ellen returned a minute later with a hefty sword taken from one of the wall displays downstairs.

"Appropriate," Carol said, covering Ellen with the gun. "Now, get working and we'll—"

The laird's ghost had covered the distance between Craig and Carol in three long strides and plunged both hands into her body.

"Down!" Shane shouted as Carol screamed.

The gun went off, and Craig felt something sting his left cheek. It was, he noted dispassionately, far less painful than taking a punch from Ramona. He landed on all fours as Carol fired again. This time, he heard the bullet strike stonework and ricochet. Craig looked up to see Carol's arm jerk upward, and the gun pointing at the ceiling. Tara, sprawled in cover beside the bed, was staring intently at the Englishwoman.

Alfie started to turn, groping for his gun, which he'd shoved into the elastic waistband of his khaki pants. Shane was already too close, though, and felled Alfie with a punch to what might have once been the point of the chubby man's chin. Alfie reeled backward, dropping the stone figurine, which landed on the floor with a satisfying crack. Then Shane quickly takes the man's gun and shoots him point blank.

Carol Bright was lying on the floor, twitching spasmodically. Tara bent and wrenched the gun from the woman's fingers.

"What do we do now, guys?" she asked.

In the corner by the door, the spirit of the Celtic warrior was now free, regarding the intruders with baleful green eyes.

CHAPTER 36

POSSESSION

"Is he coming for us?" Tara asked.

Two daggers were whirling in the air in front of her.

"Not yet," Shane said.

Craig could feel the coldness that had greeted him when he entered the Red Chamber. The shadowy apparition was unmoving, but its power seemed to increase. It was, Craig thought, probably recovering from Alfie's restraining spell.

"Will it attack, Angus?" he asked.

The dead laird did not reply. Instead, he stepped deftly around the space where the daggers spun and approached the sword ghost. The dark phantom ignored him, still glaring at the Americans and Ellen. But when Angus reached out a beckoning hand, the green eyes turned his way. At the same moment, the red-haired boy materialized from the wall near the window and rushed to join McIvor.

"Come," the ghostly laird said. "Come, and we shall both be at rest."

The boy, nodding and grinning as usual, spoke to the warrior's spirit. The dark ghost did not hesitate. It shook its head and swatted McIvor's hand aside. But this did not deter McIvor, who stepped closer, reaching out with both arms outstretched. And now, Craig could see something else. The dark filaments that had previously revealed the location of the sword filled the space between McIvor and the warrior's spirit.

"You drove me to madness. Made me kill the ones I loved," McIvor said. "Now is the time for us both to make amends."

The dark specter raised the glimmering sword but was too late. McIvor gripped the man-shaped shadow and held it to him. Fiery sparks of energy flashed out as the ancient spirit strove to free itself.

"Now!" he cried. "Now, lad!"

"What the hell is going on?" Tara cried.

Craig ran forward, focusing on the contrasting figures, and grasping their minds. The unnatural coldness was intense.

"You don't have to do this," Shane said. "We can…"

Shane's voice died away, and the room grew dark. Craig had succeeded in reaching something. It was a mind of sorts, but one so distorted and simplified by centuries of rage that it barely qualified as human. At the same time, he sensed something more human. Grief. Remorse. Sadness. The soul of Angus McIvor, tortured by his sins, and desperate to move on.

"Heaven or Hell, let me go where I must go."

A vortex opened above them. As with the woman and child Craig had helped when he arrived, it beckoned him into another's life. But this time, the whirlpool of energy did not merely threaten to deluge him with commonplace joys and pains of existence. This time, he would suffer the personal hell of a man who had done the unthinkable.

A man looked up at him. A pale, round face fringed with an untidy beard. An Englishman. Lambert? Lambton? Craig couldn't recall, and it hardly mattered. The point was that the hirelings had finally found something of value. Just as the wise woman had said, there was treasure in the mound. He commanded the workman to hand him a gold trinket. Then he gazed down past the peasant at the skeletal figure.

A sword. Truly a prize for a nobleman.

He leaped down into the pit. All the while, he felt a voice, small and remote, telling him to stop, to get away, to flee this place and have the men cover the nameless remains. But it was too late for that. He unwrapped the sword and ran a finger along the leaf-shaped blade. The weapon spoke to him in a voice like thunder, a voice that shook the world. A great deluge of emotion washed over him. All morality and reason fled, and he was transformed. Free of constraint, he thought only of war, blood, and slaughter.

Killing was the only true freedom a man should know.

He did not notice that he had slashed open the workman's throat until the gush of warm blood splashed over his chest and crotch. The warrior laughed and climbed out of the pit. More pale, stupid faces looked on. He strode forward, bloody blade raised high, smiling with the thought of all he could do for the god of battles. The god of death.

Craig almost broke free from the memory, but it was too strong. It carried him along like a tsunami of cold fury until he found himself in a familiar room. A woman cowered in a corner with a small child in her arms and a girl of around six clinging to her side. The woman spoke words in a language Craig no longer understood. Her face seemed familiar, but he could not recall her name. It did not matter. She was not of his tribe.

The sword moved in his hand as if it had a will of its own. Perhaps it did. That, too, was of no importance. Only death mattered. Pleas and screams and protestations of love meant nothing. The blade came down again and again. He saw everything in the clearest detail. Angus McIvor had lived in this moment for more than five hundred years. Craig Ellison experienced every moment of his suffering in an instant.

"Can you hear me?"

A woman was looking down at him. It was the wise woman,

dark-haired and full-lipped, with a face that lent itself to caprice and flirtation. But not at this moment. Craig's mind, shattered by horror and remorse, slowly reassembled itself as strong hands sat him upright on what he now realized was a couch. The dark-haired woman was bending over him. She had one hand on his heart, and her brow was furrowed in concentration.

"Ellen?"

She smiled, took her hand away, and straightened. Craig wanted to ask her to put it back. Tara was kneeling by him, and Shane was still holding him upright.

"Did it work?" Tara asked.

"It did," Shane replied. "At least on McIvor."

Craig tried to remember. McIvor was gone. There were still many things Craig did not understand. He looked over at the window and saw a pool of shadow fading.

"The sword is still possessed, but the ghost seems inactive for now," he said. "I don't know about the laird."

He looked back at Ellen.

"What did you do?"

The woman smiled.

"Let's just say I made up for something one of my ancestors did. A woman called Mary Lennox. She gave a man some bad advice."

CHAPTER 37

AFTERMATH AND DEPARTURE

The police sealed off the Red Chamber, but the forensics team didn't take long to complete its work. Among them, Ellen and the Americans came up with a story of hearing gunshots and rushing to the room to a fight in progress. This neatly explained Craig's injuries. He'd tried to intervene but had been beaten up and nearly shot. They agreed that the Brights and the Kleists had been treasure hunters, fixated on the mound.

"Things were a bit tense," Craig told one detective, "but I never thought they'd come to all this."

The cop muttered something about "gold fever" and asked Craig for his contact information in the U.S. The autopsies would take weeks due to budgetary issues. This meant that, after taking statements from everyone concerned, the police departed. The team carefully removed the tape marked "Do Not Cross" and went back into the Red Chamber.

"Okay," Shane said. "Let's get this party started."

He dropped what looked like a regular gym bag onto the bed. It landed with a hefty thump and sank several inches into the mattress. It was lined with sheets of lead. Shane had searched the Brights' room while Ellen had called the police and had appropriated the bag. Clearly, the English ghost hunters had intended to take the sword with its guiding spirit intact.

"Is that what Stark wants?" Tara asked.

"It's what he's going to get," Shane said. "If Craig can't shift that ghost, nobody can."

Craig, whose face was only throbbing gently now, appreciated the compliment.

Ellen had procured some tools from Hamish the handyman. Tara predictably asked if she'd also had a word about lingerie. The subsequent joking relieved some of the tension. Soon, Shane was chipping away at the mortar under the windowsill slab with a chisel. There was no activity from the ghost.

"I guess you gave it something to puzzle over," Shane said when Craig mentioned this. "If he pops out, we can handle him."

While Shane worked, Craig asked Ellen some questions. Her replies were evasive. Yes, she was a descendant of the wise woman who had advised Angus to open the mound. Yes, she had contrived to put the Germans in the Red Chamber.

"Was it because you thought the ghost might attack me?" Tara asked.

"I thought," Ellen said carefully, "that the arrival of several people with paranormal abilities might destabilize things. What I didn't grasp was that, as well as you guys, the Brights were wild talents… or at least Alfie was. And I had no idea that the Kleists were after the lost Eagle."

Shane paused, gazing out of the window toward the burial mound.

"Is it under there?" he asked. "The Eagle of the Ninth Legion?"

"Who knows?" Ellen shrugged. "The point is that folks around here don't want the mound touched again. You can see why. The Romans worshipped their Eagles. The idols of the Legions embodied all the raw power of Rome. All the hopes and dreams that shaped Europe and beyond. I think other people's gods are best left alone."

Shane resumed chiseling. Tara, her daggers in hand, turned to face Ellen.

"Who are you working for? The Shadow Trust?"

Ellen smiled, made a "my lips are sealed" gesture, and got up. Looking down at Craig, she grew serious.

"This is just the beginning," she said. "My only real power is healing, but I get glimpses sometimes. Through a glass darkly, you could say. You will face a terrible choice, Craig, but you're a good man. You doubt yourself so much, as truly good men do."

She leaned forward, kissed him on the forehead, and then walked out without another word. Craig felt himself blush.

"Okaaay, I think I got it." Shane grunted.

Tara used her power to help shift the slab while the two men worked up a sweat the conventional way. Between the three of them, they removed the windowsill to expose a long, slender hollow in the stone beneath. The sword lay lengthwise, pointing into the room. It showed no sign of possession, but Craig felt a chill as the light caught the blade.

Shane brought the bag over from the bed and laid it by the window. Tara, her head down and her mouth set in a firm line, lifted the sword with her mind and deposited it. She zipped up the bag for good measure.

"Probably best to keep all hands off it," she said. "I'll take it down to the car tomorrow."

They were ahead of schedule, but a message to Stark had already produced an efficient response. They were to take the sword to Edinburgh, and some of Stark's operatives would handle it from there. Full payment plus a bonus would then be deposited in Tara's and Craig's accounts.

"No judgment here. I know it's all about the Benjamins with you guys," Shane remarked when they told him at dinner that evening. "But don't you wonder what you're helping Stark achieve?"

"Yeah," Craig said. "All the time. But we're out of our league with this stuff. Are you willing to help us find out?"

Shane forked a mouthful of steak and eggs into his mouth, chewed briefly, and swallowed.

"Good chef here. Five stars," he remarked. "And yeah, why not? When they took my car, it got personal. And I guess you two need all the help you can get."

Craig and Tara packed most of their stuff that night so they could leave early the next day. Craig shoved his worn clothes into his bags and went into the bathroom. When he emerged, Tara was standing and looking at a business card. She held it out to him, and he took it.

"It was in one of the drawers."

They had seen one like it before. It was the calling card of the Shadow Trust. But this one bore a message in neat handwriting, complete with a signature.

See you soon.

Kind regards,
Marcus

THE PENULTIMATE TRUTH

It amused Peregrine Stark to christen his underground room the Red Chamber. Unlike the Red Chamber at Castle McIvor, Stark's lair had not seen any bloodshed. But its occasional denizen—the reason for the room's existence—was far more terrifying than any mere ghost. And the color of blood served as a constant reminder of the nature of the quest.

There was another reason for the name.

The haunted sword was the penultimate item on his list. The seven items had to be obtained in the correct order, otherwise, the quest was futile. After the sword was gained, Stark had to decide upon his destiny. Even at such a late stage, he could choose to abandon this quest. Stark could live out his life as a wealthy man with a fund of knowledge and contacts to protect him from the envious and vengeful.

Or, he could continue along the path he had chosen many years ago, and thus complete the process that would transform him, and the world, forever. Death and destruction on a grand scale would merely be the first stage of the process. The ultimate aim was a world where Stark could rule as a god, and that was something he'd always felt was his destiny.

Now that he was faced with the choice, it was no choice at all.

"I have it," Stark said loudly, placing a long, slender package in the center of the table.

He opened the box carefully, removing slips of paper and

amulets that had constrained the ghost during its long journey. His agents in Britain had followed his instructions precisely. They knew better than to do otherwise. Once the forces binding the ghost were gone, he unwrapped layers of cloth, foam, and finally, oiled leather. The sword gleamed dully in the indirect light of the chamber. He laid it on the white cloth he had prepared earlier.

A gust of cold air tousled Stark's hair. A brief, subdued moan came from somewhere nearby. He smiled at the leaf-shaped blade. The ghost was striving to manifest itself against this new enemy, but such entities were powerless in the Red Chamber. Only two beings were free to act here. Stark, and the one he served.

"Do not be afraid, bold warrior," he murmured. "There will be ample time to fight and slay the outsiders when we are all as one."

Stark waited. In front of him, directly opposite the heavy vault door, was a more modest portal. This door was covered in red leather and dotted with metal studs. Stark began to wonder, as seconds ticked by, if he had made a mistake.

"This ancient sword of wrath awaits the will of Yelbeghen!" he declared. "Will the mighty one not accept my tribute?"

The red door opened slowly to reveal a black rectangle. Beyond it, stood the Other.

The figure was, Stark often thought, a perfect instance of what the poet Milton had termed "darkness visible". It had at first been like a three-dimensional shadow, but as its strength had increased, the entity had become radiant with a kind of anti-light. Stark had little interest in the physics of it, suspecting that natural laws simply did not apply. He was, however, sometimes worried that the pain the black glow inflicted on his eyes might cause permanent damage.

Still, he thought, *the flesh is fleeting, while our power and glory will be eternal. I must keep the faith.*

The Other stepped across the threshold and into the room. The being had grown more powerful with the addition of the amulet obtained from Grendon Mill. It filled the Red Chamber with a dark energy that set Stark's flesh tingling and started to leach the warmth from his body. And yet, for all its power, Stark sensed that the Other was still yearning for completion. Five sacred relics had been absorbed into the strange entity. One was present now. A seventh awaited discovery in a distant land.

"Yelbeghen," Stark intoned. "Sevenfold in glory thou wast, sevenfold in glory thou wilt be! Accept, Oh Magnificent Prince of Air and Darkness, this humble offering!"

Stark knelt, making obeisance and averting his eyes. Before, he had been able to treat the Other as almost an equal, a being of great potential but limited scope. Now, all pretense of a partnership had to end. On this day, the slave would please his master. And soon, before the turning of the year, the worshipper would become one with his god.

Check out these best-selling series from our talented authors:

GHOST STORIES

RON RIPLEY
BERKLEY STREET SERIES
MOVING IN SERIES
HAUNTED COLLECTION SERIES
DEATH HUNTER SERIES

IAN FORTEY
JIGSAW OF SOULS SERIES
CULT OF THE ENDLESS NIGHT SERIES

SUPERNATURAL SUSPENSE

A. I. NASSER
SLAUGHTER SERIES
SIN SERIES

DAVID LONGHORN
NIGHTMARE SERIES
ASYLUM SERIES

SARA CLANCY
THE BELL WITCH SERIES
BANSHEE SERIES

For a complete list of our new releases and best-selling horror books, visit ScareStreet.com or scan the QR code below!

www.ingramcontent.com/pod-product-compliance
Lightning Source LLC
Chambersburg PA
CBHW050344030726
47503CB00008B/2602

* 9 7 9 8 8 9 4 7 6 2 9 6 8 *